AF443808

Quilting Can Be Criminal

Book One of the Fiber Mavens Mysteries

By

J. Traveler Pelton

copyright © 2020
Potpourri Publishing, Limited
Mt. Vernon, OH 43050

COPYRIGHT

Quilting Can Be Criminal: Book One of the Fiber Mavens Mysteries by Traveler Pelton
Copyright© 2020

Independently published by Potpourri Publishing
Cover design by RebecaCovers
Edited by Write Useful

Printed in the United States of America
First Edition published
Books> fiction> mystery
ISBN- 9798630988409

Dedication

First, to my God and Creator, Savior and Guide, who gives us dreams and tasks, who gifts us with imagination and who breathes life into our dreams.

I dedicate with love to all those who have been to the shadowy edge of life, looked over and decided to come back and try again. I've been there, I came back. May you keep the warmth and wealth of love in your hearts always. Love is what keeps us whole.

I dedicate it to my ancestors who walked the Red Road before me. Someday we will all walk the Skylands together. Until then our hearts beat with the drum of unity and peace.

May God grant us the courage to live with whatever life sends us and overcome trials always with His peace.

Finally, to my readers, because a story isn't a story until someone else hears it; it is simply a phantasm, a dream in the maker's head. You make it live when you read it and for just a few brief moments, our imaginations combine and that's when magic is still alive...

Other Books by Traveler Pelton
Spiritual Works
- God Wanted to Write a Bestseller
- Big God, Little Me
- Lenten Stories for God's Little Children
- Natural Morning
- Ninety Days to The God Habit
- Tales for Advent and Christmas
- His Path Is Mine

Christian Literary Science Fiction
The First Oberllyn Family Trilogy: The Past
- The Oberllyn's Overland: 1855-1862
- Terrorists, Traitors and Spies 1900-1990
- Rebooting the Oberllyn's 2015-2020

The Second Oberllyn Family Trilogy: The Present
- The Infant Conspiracy
- Kai Dante's Stratagem
- The Obligation of Being Oberllyn

The Third Oberllyn Family Trilogy: The Future
- To Protect One's Own
- The Importance of Family Ties
- Kith and Kin, Together Again

In Collaboration with T. Bear Pelton:
- Clan Falconer's War
- The Rise of the Rebellion
- Changeling's Clan
- Forged in Water and Fire

The Fiber Mavens Mystery Series
Quilting Can be Criminal

Other Authors Associated with Potpourri Publishing

Lynette Spencer of Write Useful
- <u>Sewing on a Budget</u>
- <u>Vegetarian Cooking on a Budget</u>

Dan Pelton
<u>The Majestic Spectrum of God's Love</u>

Preface

"Doctor, you have to be wrong. She's not old enough to die." The young man leaned forward in his seat in the doctor's office. "Mom didn't have any symptoms or anything."

"I'm sorry, son. Your mom's had a hard life. She did all the best she could, but she has pancreatic cancer. There is little to nothing I can do about it."

"Then treat her."

"There isn't any treatment at this stage except for palliatives; keep her comfortable, get hospice involved. Her cancer will spread slowly at first and then more rapidly. She won't be uncomfortable for a few months yet, but I'm afraid your mom has about six months of good life left, and then she'll need to go on painkillers to control discomfort and she'll live about six weeks after that. There is nothing anyone can do to stop it."

"But how did this happen? She was fine last summer when I came home from college and just said she had to take some treatments."

"We tried removing the tumors. We did. But your mom worked all those years exposed to solvents and she smoked all those years and she had diabetes; it all just caught up with her."

"If we hadn't been so poor, she could have afforded better food," fumed the young man. "Had dad not copped out on us, she'd never have had to go work in that factory."

"That's all past history, son. There's nothing we can do now except make sure her last days are happy ones."

"But I just got out of college and I wanted to be able to help her now. She's worked all these years for me; I want to show her some gratitude and I can't in six months. She deserves years of simpler living."

"I'm sorry. Think, man, you learned about this stuff in school. You know there is nothing science can do, it's pretty much all palliative now. You can get a second opinion, but if it were me, I'd take her home to live and allow her to just enjoy what time she has, maybe take some short trips, a quiet place to be."

The young man bent his head. "All that study, all that work, I took extra jobs to avoid debt so I would be able to help Mom as soon as I graduated. I'm in a great place now, she's so proud of me. She's been so good to me. Now she'll go back to that crappy little apartment above the grocery." He shook his head. "Well, I can support her now. I'll see she doesn't want for anything."

"Your mom is on disability now. When she got the diagnosis originally, I was able to push that through so she could stop working. She's quit smoking, as of six months ago." The doctor paused, then added, "I wanted to talk to you both about hospice care."

The young man shook his head and shuddered. His mother came out of the exam room to meet him and he drove her home, back to her little apartment.

"Why didn't you tell me, Mom?" he asked softly.

"I wanted you to graduate and not come tearing home to rescue me," she said flatly. "You earned that degree with your stint in the army and you did grand and I am so proud of you. Someday, you'll find a nice girl and settle down and have kids and be able to take good care of them and you promise me you'll not run away from them like your dad, you hear me? I talked to the social worker at the hospital and she says Hospice has a nice home for folks to go to. At first, you're in your own apartment but as you get worse, you sort of move to more care needed part until it's over. I won't have to climb any stairs or anything. I won't have to cook or run errands. I can just watch TV and maybe putter a bit in their flower beds. I have always wanted a flower bed again. I can take my plants with me."

"Mom, how about if I find us a place without stairs and I take care of you?"

"Now, don't go dumping your career because of me. You need to finish what you started twelve years ago. I'll be gone soon, and it doesn't make any sense to uproot you. I'd appreciate it if you visited and maybe found time for a girlfriend? Grandkids would be good to think about,"

Her son set his jaw. He took a deep breath and answered quietly. "I'm going to take care of you, Mom. Don't worry. I will. And I believe I will just take care of some other things as well. Don't fret yourself. The right girl will come along, and the right things will be done."

Chapter 1

Miriam Miller and Lydia Fisher rode together to their jobs in downtown Lyonsville. Their brother Eli drove the carriage for them; he was tasked with going into the market for his mam, and he would drop his sisters off to their jobs and return later to fetch them to their homes. Their kinder were being watched by their own older sisters. Miriam and Lydia enjoyed working during the tourist season. Not only were they paid, but the employee discount also came in handy for buying needed fabric for their family's clothes.

It was a lovely fall day, leaves turning and making the burning bush hedge in front of the public library change from a quiet green to a vibrant red. Driving slowly down Main street, they saw the librarian, Mrs. Olsen, unlocking the front doors to the library as they passed; she nodded and smiled. Miriam waved back. The Public Library was popular in Lyonsville; the librarian and her helpers and volunteers kept it tidy and in order. Mrs. Olsen had several computers set up so local folks could access the web. There were children's programs and adult programs that ran on different evenings. The downstairs had been turned into three meeting rooms, an office, and storage. Colorful bulletin boards greeted anyone using the rooms with the announcements of the week and rules. Upstairs, the library had a reading room full of magazines on neat shelves, a youth room where kids could come and do artwork, a children's section complete with a playroom of educational toys with regularly scheduled read-to-me hours. Then there were the stacks, books and books and books in all different subjects, over twelve thousand and access through the computer to thousands more available online. With the blessing of the city council and the library board, Mrs. Olsen had a lending library of tablets for seniors that could be loaded with books from the big state library, and many a senior decided after using one for a while they had to have one of their own. Through a special program, they were able to get a tablet and case for a modest amount, then they took a class in how to access it from the library and download six books a week for themselves. Mrs. Olsen was gratified that the program worked so well, as it was her brainchild. Grants and gifts from local industries paid for the extras that the library operating funds could not, and due to public interest and support, it was a very nice, up to date little library important to the people of Lyonsville and enjoyed by many of the residents, English and Amish alike.

Eli noted as he drove his horse towards the shops that the traffic had calmed down since school had restarted; most tourists had left. Eli pulled the buggy behind the Fiber Maven's yarn shop where Lydia worked; her boss, Alyssa Martin, had gone to the trouble of putting up a small shelter and tie-out for horses since there were so many Amish customers. She had installed an outdoor water spigot so the horses could be given water while their owners shopped and three black stock buckets were hanging next to the faucet. Eli grabbed a bucket and went to get some water for the horse as his sisters climbed down. Miriam quietly said to her sister, "I'll see you at lunch. About one?"

"Ya, the rush should be over then, and we can eat in the employee room," replied Lydia. "I'll put our lunches in the refrigerator."

"We had a new shipment come in last night," Miriam said as she waited for Lydia. "I suspect I'll be putting it away this morning." They walked into the back door together. "We have that new Beginning Quilt group coming in at eleven. It's always good to help others learn." Miriam continued.

As they chatted, they hung their bonnets and shawls in the break room, straightened their aprons and checked in, splitting and going one to the left and one to the right from the shared room. "And we have a Knit and Kneel group starting this afternoon. I do enjoy those," answered Lydia.

Alyssa and her sister Suzanne had inherited the building together when their parents had passed. Their mother had had a fabric store on one side of the building with the other side for storage. When the sisters inherited it, they expanded the building. Now there was a widened connection area in between where there was a bathroom that opened into both stores and a back room that had become a joint employee room. The storeroom stretched on either side of the back of both stores and the offices for the two stores were at either end of the storage area. It felt as if there were several buildings connected. Upstairs were two apartments.

Suzanne's son, Alan Martin, had the apartment on the right and acted as a night watchman most the time; the other apartment was rented out to old Mrs. Harmony, who had lived there alone with her poodle and Himalayan cat from the time their mother had owned the building. Mrs. Harmony knew everyone and everything going on. She was still a faithful attendee to yarn groups and church. She was an avid knitter, so much so that last summer, she had yarn bombed the bench in front of the Fiber Mavens' Shoppe in a lovely red, white and blue for the Fourth of July celebrations and would have knitted or crocheted around the tree trunks had she not been stopped in time. As it was, and to make it all match, the Yarn Sisters group had yarn bombed the other two benches on the block for July 4th so they'd match. After the holiday, they quietly took the playful results off the benches at the request of City Council – and it was a request since two of the council member's wives were members of the yarn group and they honestly didn't want to cause a town-wide incident with their wives in the middle, especially as the little town had a long memory and there was an election next year.

When Alyssa and her sister had taken over the building after their mom's passing, they had decided to be synergistic and make one side of the building a fiber shop, offering yarns, fibers for spinning, knitting, crocheting and needlework supplies. Alyssa was an experienced knitter and spinner and kept a wheel here in the store available for quiet moments. She offered classes in spinning, dyeing, knitting and had two other ladies help with crocheting and needlework classes.

Suzanne had updated, enlarged, and renamed her mother's fabric store, calling it Fabric Avalanche and added a large, brightly lit classroom that both businesses used to hold groups. There was always a quilt on a quilting frame to which anyone could take a moment or two and add a few stitches; when it was done, it was bound and raffled for a local charity. They'd raised over three thousand dollars for the local Amish school and the local women's shelter that way, and women vied for the honor of piecing the top that would be the next charity round robin.

On either side of this building, their husbands had bought lots and expanded the building to add storerooms in the back and a business to each side. Alyssa's husband, Thom, operated Thom's Hobbies on the right side. He carried anything radio-controlled and science/techy. Most of the men and boys in town were in there at some time. He sold everything RC, be it robots, trains, planes, or hovercraft; lots of science kits, electronic parts and gizmos; and, for some odd reason, six jars of penny candies upfront by the cash register: butterscotch drops, lemon drops, root beer barrels, pink wintergreens, lollipops, and jawbreakers in cinnamon so strong it was hard to keep them in your mouth; indeed, most kids didn't for long – they licked them for hours instead, getting sticky and pink in the process. There was a mason jar with a slot in the lid to put your pennies in, and the proceeds went to the local 4-H club for their yearly fair booth supplies. Thom always sponsored the booth at the fair.

On the left side of the ladies' building, Suzanne's husband, Mike, and their son, Alan, operated Not Your Normal Antique Store. It had an extremely eclectic feel, not just old furniture, glassware, and pictures, but unusual books and odd memorabilia. For instance, Mike had the first articulated prosthetic hand, which was rumored to be haunted and to move around the store by itself at night. He had a missionary cabinet organ made to be carried from place to place, unpacked and used for evangelistic meetings; there were a six-foot-high walking spinning wheel and a theramin that you played by just getting your hands near it, and, for some reason only known to Thom, an embalmed cat. You never quite knew what he was going to add to the mix that seemed part museum, part store, and was very much loved by tourists and townspeople alike. All four businesses filled one block of Main Street.

Behind the businesses, the lot had been set up as a small picnic area complete with a parking lot for cars by the building, a loading area and a side area with trees, a couple of picnic tables, a tie out for buggies, and a water spigot so the Amish could water their horses.

The Amish knew there was a bucket kept up by the back door, just inside.

The Amish and English got along well in Lyonsville, the main street of the town being a blend of English and Amish stores and shops. People coming off route 30 would turn up Main Street, passing the first two blocks of neatly maintained, mostly white-painted, single-family homes. Several homes had front porches and flowerbeds. One or two had twinkly lights on topiaries by their front doors. There was one odd Pepto-Bismol pink cottage in the row; every year, it gave the zoning board a conniption to realize they could not do anything about it as it was owned by the mother of the owner of the largest company in the township and he was not going to allow them to make his mom, 89-year-old Mildred Snipes, upset. He promised he'd paint it a quieter shade once she passed on and he inherited it. She seemed immortal to the Zoning Board.

The pink house, as everyone called it, was on the corner of Main and Pickman Street, and if you crossed the street and continued down the sidewalk, there was another ivory-colored house and then one of the two bed and breakfasts in town. The owners had bought a large house and the lot on either side, fenced it all into one large yard with picket fencing, put a pool in the back, and planted lots of climbing roses on the fence. The front yard was a rose garden as well, with flagstone walks running through the flowers and around to the back; on a warm summer day, the smell was intoxicating. They always seemed to have flowers blooming; there were not only roses but a variety of flowers planted so something was always in bloom somewhere. If you walked through the front arbor, you'd see a large two-story home, a wraparound porch populated with several rocking chairs, a glider swing, and small tables that had checker games or decks of cards on them. Beth and Franklin Stevens ran the Rose Garden Bed and Breakfast, and they were famous for their plate-sized cinnamon rolls at breakfast.

A visitor walking past Rose Garden B&B came first to Ricci's Restaurant, which was famous for its ravioli in eighteen different combinations and Italian ices in strange flavors like Orange Mango Banana and Lime Whiz. Across the street, Fred's Finer Diner served traditional Amish food along with marvelous baked goods from

Hannah's Bakery. The two restaurants enjoyed a friendly rivalry; Tuesdays seemed to be Italian night in town, and on Thursday's Amish noodles over mashed potatoes were popular with local folk. Next in line came the public library followed by an old building that no one seemed to know whether to preserve or tear down: it had been the courthouse once and folks thought it ought to be preserved, but it had gone through several reincarnations as a grange and a duplex and now sat empty and sad.   The Sheriff's station on the left, with the post office and First Bank on the right, with a parking lot in between made up the third block of Main street. Hannah's Bakery was operated in a small shop attached to Fred's by Hannah Byler and her three daughters and was a quiet, unassuming place. Every morning at 6 they opened the doors and the most enticing odors would emanate from the front door, luring people in by their noses as they walked by to work. Their Muffins on Monday's always sold out by nine, and the locals knew to get there early.

Continuing down the street, Finian's Fine Furniture stood on the third corner, carrying all furniture that was not Amish; owned and operated by Finian Ippish II, having moved into the store when he was fourteen and buying it from his father's estate when the old man died. He had a bachelor's apartment over his store, the same one his father had dwelled in after his mother died. Finian was a loner, a sort of reclusive man who was much into conspiracy theories and "real wood furniture", as he called it, "not this paste-board stuff from China." He was respected by the folk in the town for being honest, enlarging his father's furniture business and adding staff. He had a degree in fine arts. He longed to be a museum curator. He settled for talking to Thom and helping him find acquisitions for the antique/museum store. In turn, Thom had him over for dinner once a week and they watched Antiques Roadshow with a passion.

The Getalong Café was operated by Jane and Adam Long and served up pizza, cheeseburgers, even vegetarian burgers, fries and salads, a little of every kind of American food. They had photos of famous folks who had eaten here since 1955 when it first opened; from Eisenhower posing with the original owners to Travis Tritt smiling as he and his men stopped in their big tour bus on the way to the performance at the state fair, effectively filling up the entire back

parking lot with one vehicle. The décor had been changed now and
then but had finally been restored to the original checkered
tablecloths on round tables, with a long bar and tall chrome stools.
Their two kids, Mikey and David, bussed the tables after school and
in the summer.

Across the street on this block sat St. Edwards Park that
adjoined the schoolyard in the back. Children were allowed to go over
to the new playground in the park at recess since the school grounds
didn't have enough land for a good, all-ages playground and had
settled for a fenced-in smaller one for the "littles", Kindergarten
through second grade. It was a big thing for kids in third grade to
move to the park playground with the "bigs." The school was
progressive, with raised flower and vegetable beds, a greenhouse, and
a small observatory. The children grew vegetables that they took
home to their families, and any excess was donated to the local
church pantry to be given out to whoever needed food. The school
had hired an older Amish gentleman to teach the children agriculture,
and many of them ended up lifetime gardening enthusiasts. The
observatory was open weekend evenings for the public, and the
middle and high school students took classes that met in the evenings.

Back on Main Street, Dave's Market took up the last available
block on the left side. The store manager, David Hershberger, carried
all the regular groceries, plus bulk foods and some general store
items; they sold fishing worms and lures, they had camping supplies
and souvenirs, and an Urgent Care operated next to the pharmacy at
the rear of the store. Marti Davis was the nurse practitioner and her
husband, Liam, was the town pharmacist. Across the street, the BP
gas station was run by a perpetually engaged couple, Francis May and
Stuart Hahler. Francis was an incredible mechanic; her husband-to-be
ran the gas station books and kept inventory but never got his hands
particularly dirty. Francis, on the other hand, never seemed to be able
to get all the oil and grease out of her nails or off her face. Next was a
coffee shop that had the best biscotti and donuts in town, run by an
older gentleman, a widower named Reggie who simply called his
shop Coffee. Next to Coffee squatted the bookstore, Reflections,
operated by an older hippy lady, Melody Bibby. She played sitar
music, served tea in odd flavors, had couches and chairs to sit in as

you checked out books, and the back half of her shop, facing the back alley, was the town's laundromat and tanning salon. The final building held Armstrong Hardware, operated by a young military veteran, Matt Armstrong, who was also a volunteer firefighter, which was good since the last full block was the fire department. Matt's sister Casey was a Social worker who worked for the county Family Services. She sometimes stopped by his store to pick up things to repair something at their mom's house: Mrs. Armstrong was perpetually breaking this or that at home. Folks said she alone was a good reason for her son to own a hardware store. They thought Casey ought to have been a home handyman instead of working in Child Protection. She could just about fix anything, thanks to her mom. In the same building as the hardware was Suzy's Beauty Salon and Spa, which actually had a salt room for those of more esoteric tastes, a manicurist named Ben, and a masseuse who worked part-time named Melissa. Ben was a slight man who was an avid jujitsu practitioner. Melissa taught piano on the side; she had incredibly strong hands. She also volunteered as a fireman. On occasion, she helped farmers with haying, finding that working in the outdoors was exhilarating. She is at least a foot taller than Ben. He doesn't seem to mind. Suzy was known to not be a gossip: what was shared in the salon stayed in the salon, and many women in town found her comforting to visit.

Several of the side streets have small businesses as well, and once the main street dead-ended into the crossroad, Winchester Avenue, the "fancy houses" lined the street. Several dated back a hundred years, full of bric-a-brac and formal porches; big mansions that boasted brick sidewalks and stained-glass windows in the entrances. A visitor would see large oak trees that buckled the sidewalks along this road, making it shady and somewhat treacherous; some of the houses had old ironwork fencing, others low cut hedges. Here the second bed and breakfast was situated on the corner of Winchester and Marble lane. The building chosen to be a Bed and Breakfast was huge, imposing, and formal, with ironwork fencing and gates. If the ancient trees in the front yards could talk, they'd reminisce of parties on the patio, brick streets, horses and carriages, long dresses and beaver hats. Sandra and Joseph Michaels, the owners, had retired from the craziness of being Chicago CFO's in their respective companies to this bed and breakfast. They had constructed a formal garden, with a labyrinth made of short hedges that ended in a covered gazebo holding a ball fountain, constantly spinning in the back yard. The swimming pool was enclosed and had replaced a stable on the side; there were benches in shady spots all around the building, and the understated elegance of an older era showed in the fireplaces in each room, the deep claw-footed tubs in each bathroom, the antiques in the formal dining hall and living room. Their morning spread was a sight to behold, usually no less than three kinds of quiche, hot homemade croissants, fruit salads, coffee in differing flavors, pastilitos filled with homemade jams and cream. Once a month they hosted a mystery dinner that was incredibly popular with tourists and, offseason, with the residents of the town. They served dinner as part of the mystery night and people were encouraged to wear costumes matching the theme. Many locals spent wedding anniversaries here; their anniversary suite was private, comfortable and their wedding or anniversary package included fine chocolates, a complimentary bottle of champagne, and a basket of hot homemade bread rolls and local spreadable cheeses. A small gift shop carrying local homemade jams, jellies, and small Amish crafts was to the left as you entered. The Michael's named their bed and breakfast Oakhurst Manor.

Standing in front of the Manor and looking back down Main Street a visitor would see a friendly small-town street lined with alternating dogwoods, flowering pears, and crabapple trees. The streetlamps were Colonial in style and came on most of the time at dusk. Between the trees were either a wastebasket and bench or a raised flower bed, lovingly tended by the local garden club. The street lamps, during the summer months, had alternating flowering baskets of pink, white, or blue petunias, with banners hung underneath advertising the different organizations in town, from the Rotary Club to the churches, to Kiwanis, to the 4-H clubs and the extension office, the Chamber of Commerce and visitor's bureau, the school, AAA, VFW, the Moose, Elks, and the Weight Watchers club. All the banners were green except the two for the churches; those were purple.

The First Church was just beyond the cemetery. Huge old oaks and maples sheltered the cemetery, and each family seemed to have their own little plot, some decorated elaborately, most more simply with spring bulbs or the occasional small flowering shrub. Pastor Malachi Primo, his wife Lizbeth lived in the parish house beside the church. Services were promptly at ten Sunday mornings, with Sunday school following to allow for him driving to his other church, a larger one, in a nearby town and being there for noon services. Most weeks he made it home by three. He and his wife are high church in heart, but they tone it down for the little town. Pastor Primo still wore robes, there were still candles, but the litany was shorter and the homily friendlier. He never preached outside the pulpit. The church held frequent fundraisers for missions and the church ladies were active in helping those locally who they saw as less fortunate.

At the First Church, they had prayer meetings on Wednesdays at 6 so all the stores promptly closed at five since just about everyone except the Amish attended meetings at First Church. There was a group that operated a house church that meets on Saturday mornings, eating brunch first, studying and then eating lunch together before going out and spending time at the local church aid society where they assisted in handing out food to those in need in spite of doctrinal differences with First Church. They occasionally could be counted on to help people with an overdue rent check or utility bill; they would help folks move from one home to another and seemed really nice people; just thought of as a little odd. They always could be counted on to come to work bees to pretty up the town or help someone out who found themselves in a jam. No one disliked them; everyone was pretty much cordial to the home church folks; they just seem to have some odd ideas and don't mean any harm, and this is America.

Sheriff Erick Black was proud of his town, and his deputy Brad Malcolm would deliberately make sure he would be in the park during recess at the school. He drove slowly around, watched the kids, occasionally stopped to do some paperwork until the recess period was over. Kids easily ran up to the car and talked. He knew all of them.

On this pretty fall day, Lydia entered the yarn store just as her boss was turning over the Open sign. "Good morning, Lydia," beamed Alyssa, as always smiling as she came back to the register. "I put your latest creation in the front window, and we just got in a new order of Seven Sister's yarns and I'd like you to price and arrange them over there on the left side where I made space by the other exotics. I can't believe I was able to get that color everyone's been asking about, the variegated blue, green, teal skeins. It's just a gorgeous merino, baby yak mix that you will not believe. And see what I found over the weekend? I actually got some vicuna. It's going right up here by the register so I can keep an eye on it. Feel how soft it is." She held out a twenty-five-gram ball to Lydia.

"That's the stuff that's made from those mountain animals, yah?"

"Absolutely. It's three hundred dollars a ball."

"What! Who is going to spend that?" gasped Lydia, quickly handing the ball back to Alyssa as if it were hot.

"You might be surprised, but maybe not. You know Allison Drummel, whose husband Alex runs the bank? She wants to get some to try out. I told her I'd try to get it but that it would be pricey. She read some articles about vicuna sports coats costing $21,000 or some such thing so she was going to make a scarf for her husband for his birthday. She told me she might not be able to get him a coat but least she can do is make a scarf. Nothing's too good for her husband. After all, he got her that Prius she wanted. She wants four balls of it."

"She will spend twelve hundred dollars for yarn? Mighty fancy stuff, I'd say," frowned Lydia. "On another note, it looks like we have eight signed up for the learn to crochet class and nine for the intermediate knitter's group."

"Excellent! I always like to teach those groups. Fun to be around others of like interests. I'll get these notions hung up from this box, you start on the yarn."

"Sounds like a plan," smiled her assistant, taking the box with her and heading to the shelves.

Over at Fabric Avalanche, Suzanne and Miriam were just getting the shop set up for customers. Miriam had cut off and set aside a lovely dark green length to make her two little girls dresses this week. She got a good employee discount. She also made quilt samples for the shop and had unpacked a new lap quilt she had completed the night before to be hung up as an example for the next quilting class. Just as they were getting it put up on the quilt clamps by the classroom door and were making sure it was straight, along with the sign-up sheet beside it, deputy Malcolm came in the shop.

"Morning ladies," he greeted them. "Wie gehts?"

Miriam smiled. "Your Dutch is getting much better. And we are fine, yah?"

"To what do we owe the honor of Lyonsville's most eligible bachelor coming to a fabric store?" asked Suzanne as she climbed down the step stool.

"Don't know about eligible but needed your expertise. What does this signify?" He held up a patchwork block.

"Well, that pattern is called Broken Dishes. It's normally made into a runner and given to newlyweds as a wish that their dishes will always be full and not break," Miriam smiled. "Are you taking up quilt making?"

"No, it was found at the scene of a crime."

"Excuse me?" gasped Suzanne. "Crime? What sort of crime?"

"Last night sometime, the front window of Ricci's Restaurant was broken, and this was wrapped around the rock that broke the window. It's pretty, those nice green and white colors and all, but whoever broke the window was up to no good. Nothing appears stolen, just vandalism. I don't think a kid would have taken the trouble to make a quilt square to waste this way. I've seen enough of this quilt making stuff to know it takes time and skill to make one like this. Shame to waste it this way."

Miriam took the square, holding it in its evidence bag, turning it over and studying. She handed it to Suzanne who did the same, then handed it to Brad. "Nice neat stitches, handmade as well, and cut out with pinking shears so it won't ravel. Yes, whoever made this knew what they were doing. And they knew the square names and such – choosing Broken Dishes to break a window on a restaurant – that's sort of telling, isn't it?" she observed.

"What are you thinking?" asked the deputy.

"I'm not certain. Suzanne, what do you think?"

Suzanne took the square back from Brad and studied it well. "If they were trying to make a statement, Broken Dishes seems to me to have been what they were planning but didn't get to do. They broke a window, not a dish. Unless they were interrupted and didn't get to break any dishes? At any rate, whoever did this was not an amateur. They knew how to sew, how to piece. Let me check something." She went over to the solid colored fabrics and held the piece up.

"Appears to me they used this, this and this bolt – see the fabric matches up in weave and color? So either they bought that fabric here or at one of the other dozens of stores who stock this brand. The big Walmart and the chain stores don't carry this quality of fabric. They buy cheaper. Only quilt stores carry fabric with this quality. I don't think it was here, however. See the darker green? Our bolt hasn't been touched. We just put it out this morning." Suzanne took a moment while she wrote down something.

"And the lighter green I just cut off the first piece this morning, here it is. There have been some of the ivory sold off that bolt," observed Miriam.

"This is the name of the jobber who brings us our fabric that comes in solids. If you call him, he might be able to tell you what other stores in the area carry this fabric. It's going to be a lot of footwork for you." Suzanne gave the paper she'd written on to Brad.

"That's why we get the big bucks," he joked. "Thank you for your help."

The deputy left the store. Miriam looked at Suzanne. "Can you imagine a quilting criminal in our town?"

Chapter 2

"I'm so glad to see you, son!" explained Mrs. Clamons as she opened the door to the apartment. "And who are these young men?"

"These are my friends Matthew and Dave and Tony and Mike," her son replied. "And this is moving day."

"Excuse me?" she asked.

"You've been cooped up too long in this old place. Right now, I'm taking you down to Mildred's house for a nice visit and when you get back, you are going to have such a surprise. In fact, let's drive around a little while. Some of the fall colors are stunning."

"Well, I haven't seen Mildred in a long time," she said. "And I do appreciate it, but I was going to work on a lap quilt. I'm doing the quilting on it and I hope to do the binding by the end of the week. And I have these pieces all cut-out and ready to be fitted on my next quilt That fabric you brought me is just lovely. Such pretty, Christmassy colors."

"Why not just bring your sewing basket along and the pieces and piece it at Mildred's?" he suggested. "It's a pretty day out, and we'll take the long way so you can see all the fall flowers."

"That is tempting. I hate to run just when you've brought company. Do you boys want some tea? I baked oatmeal cookies."

"Don't worry, Mrs. Clamons. We'll be fine and we'll be all done by the time you get back," asserted the one Toby had introduced as Dave.

"Done with what?" she asked.

"Oh, nothing of any import, Mom," interjected her son quickly. "Are these all the pieces?"

"Yes, just put them in my bag right there. Now did you tell Mildred I'm coming?"

"I did and she is all a bustle about it. She's got tea ready. She is looking forward to a good chat. Let me help you with that sweater."

Toby helped his mother put on a sweater, picked up her sewing box, stash bag, and purse, then assisted her down the stairs. He settled her into her pumpkin-colored bug.

"This dear old car. I don't know how long I'll be able to drive it," she said fondly, patting the dash. "Been through a lot with this old car. It's been Old Faithful to me."

"You've had it at least as long as I've been out of high school," remarked her son as he backed out the driveway. "Did you know there is another one in town?"

"What? Oh, you mean the new pastor's wife's car. No, hers is automatic. Mine's stick shift. The same color though." She sighed, "Talking to my doctor. He suggested I sign my car over to you so you could take over the driving for me. I get so tired of going in for groceries sometimes."

"We can do that later, Mom. The doctor I work for is letting me use his blue van for some errands. I catch a ride into work with Mike. I can still drive you around."

"It would be better to have a car of your own."

"I suspect so. I'll get around to that. By the way, what pattern are you doing?"

"You know the quilt I made years ago, that one that you had on your bed and that I won first place at the fair showing?? It was like a map of our town. A museum bought it and I used the money from it to get your braces. Our insurance wouldn't cover them, and you did have the biggest gap in your teeth. The quilt sold for enough to pay for the braces and get us into our apartment over the store. I've lived there now for fifteen years or more. Well, I missed that quilt. I can't exactly copy it, but I'm doing one like it in different colors. It will be a good one to give my first grandchild with, once you get around to having one, you or your brothers."

"Do they ever come 'round?"

"Not often. Last time Troy was here, he asked for some quilt blocks to give his wife to make into pillows and I had a couple of extras he took. As for Liam, I see him when I go pick up prescriptions. He has such a sweet wife. And Matthew, well, last I saw him he blew up all over about how I'd abandoned him as a child.

I didn't, you know. None of them grew up here and no knowing what nonsense your dad put in their head when he took him off."

Changing the subject, Toby asked, "How many blocks have you got to make?"

"Well, you know I always make two of each block so I can choose the nicest for the quilt and use the others as throw pillows. I might make more than one of this quilt, I don't know. I have six cut out of this pretty pattern. I gave Troy three other blocks."

"Will you have any leftover from the quilt when it's done?"

"I always do, and I eventually use them up. Why?" she replied.

Her son paused. "You know, my friend Kyle has an online store and makes some good money on the side and he just sells refurbished outdoor plastic playsets. What if I set up a store to sell your extra quilt blocks? I bet they'd sell good and you'd be able to have a little spending money. Disability, you don't get much on that. The extra income would come in handy."

"Oh, land now, son, who would buy an old woman's quilt blocks?"

"You would be surprised. If you have any finished, why don't you give them to me? If they don't sell in a week or so, I'd bring them back, you could still make pillows out of them for gifting. If they do, you have some extra money. How about it?"

"That sounds sensible." She smiled, "I have a good son. Oh! Look at those fall mums? Aren't they stunning?"

Toby slowed his car way down as he drove his mother through the best of the fall scenery and they ended up at the Pepto-Bismol house where Mildred was waiting. He dropped Marie Clamons off, told her he would be back in three hours and left them to visit. He drove back to the apartment over the store and helped his friends pack up all of his mother's worldly possessions, which did not amount to all that much, and the friends drove out to a little house on a country backroad, sandwiched between two Amish farms. There, they quickly went inside where several ladies were waiting to help set the house back up.

"This is such a cool idea," enthused one lady, a nurse where Toby worked. "Does your mom have any idea?"

"No, I've thrown some hints, but she has no idea. She's always wanted just a little place of her own, and I got a really good deal on this house. It didn't take much fixing up and I can't thank you all enough for helping," he said. "Two bedrooms, one up, one down. I'm moving into the up one, her into the bottom one. She has a kitchen, bath, living room with a fireplace, and the bonus room we have set up with the sewing machine and shelves for her stash. Did you get the fabric?"

Helen, another nurse, nodded. "I went into the quilt shop and when I explained a little of what we were doing, they gave me a bunch of fat quarters from last season, and I bought backing and a roll of batting and pillow forms. It's all on the shelves in there already. But why a treadle machine?"

"That was her machine when I was a kid," he grinned. "I picked it up from the person who'd bought it fifteen years ago. I took it to the sewing machine repairman over in Charm and it works like a new machine. Can't wait till she sees it. She sewed all the clothes I wore except for my jeans on that machine."

"Well, that's one well put together sewing room," remarked Alice, the first nurse. "You can come over anytime and build me one. I've got just her stash to add to it now. It's all cotton so far so I've got it organized by color. Is the kitchen unpacked?"

"Yes, we've added her plates and such to the cupboards, and that Corelle set you got is just right to blend in. Has she ever had a dishwasher before?" asked Alice.

"Not that I know of; is the bed made up?" asked Toby.

She nodded, "I found this quilt at the house and added it. Mike, out in my car are some flowers. Bring them in?"

"Sure," he replied and left out the front door. For over an hour, the friends charged around, arranging, settling things into place, adding little touches to make things easier to get to, simpler to keep neat, cozier to see. Simple prints were hung on the walls, along with some samplers she'd had in her apartment and photos of her and her sons. A metal rick was set up and filled with firewood and a basket of tinder. Throw rugs were attached to the wood floors so she would not slip, then with nursing eyes, the women went from room to room measuring to be sure a walker could get through. Finally, they decided it was pretty well done.

"There, furniture in place, dishes unpacked, clothing in the dresser. I put her house plants all in the south bow window in the kitchen. Where'd you get that cute little dining room set?" asked Helen.

"Amish friend of mine owns a secondhand store. It fits just right." Toby looked around. Alice took the flower arrangements Mike had brought in and sat one on the kitchen table, one on the living room coffee table and a bud vase by her chair.

"Well, I moved my stuff upstairs last night, so I'm settled in too. Wait, just minute." He looked around. "Here it is." He set a well-worn Bible on a small stand by the rocking chair by the window next to the bud vase with a red carnation in it and a pair of reading glasses. "There. I think it's about as perfect as I can make it. Thank you, everyone. I'm going to go get Mom."

"I've put a casserole in the oven, and the gelatin salad's in the fridge along with a chocolate pie, just like you asked. You do realize that's not very balanced a meal? OK, well, it ought to be ready when you bring her in. Oh! I wish I could be here to see her face!" exclaimed Helen with a smile of satisfaction. "I hope when my kids grow up they're as thoughtful as you are."

"I'll bring you all over for dinner this weekend. Mom's not much for fussing but she'll want to thank you for your part in this," he smiled. "Again, can't thank you enough."

"Well, the fire is laid so you can light it when she gets here. Ought to be cozy," said Matt from where he was squatting beside the fireplace. "It's a grand thing you're doing for your mom."

"She's everything to me," Toby replied. "Now for the big reveal."

"Well, let's just get our things and you can lock up," said Alice. "She's going to be tired and this is going to be overwhelming enough without us being here. God bless, Toby."

"You too, Alice."

His friends left. Toby drove back to the shocking pink house, retrieved his mother and they both drove quietly past the old apartment.

"Son, you forgot to turn in at the parking lot." she admonished. "Are you needing to go shopping? It's getting dark and I don't like to be getting home after dark. The stairway light has been burned out for weeks and I've not been able to get the landlord to replace it. He keeps forgetting."

"No, Mom." He replied. "We're needing to go on a little side trip first."

"Where?"

"Did you have a good time at Mildred's?"

"Don't change the subject. I'm not senile yet," she said pertly. "And yes, I did, but where are we going?"

"I wanted to show you something," he answered.

"Are we going to look at more flowers? It's getting towards dusk."

"Well, sort of. We're almost there."

They drove another couple of miles in silence. Toby pulled into a little cape cod cottage, white with green trim, with a rose trellis over the walkway gate. The lawn had been freshly mowed. There was a large tree off-center in the front yard and a forest behind it.

"I haven't been out here in years," exclaimed his mother. "Not since that awful day we lost it. Whoever owns it might not like us sitting in their driveway blocking it. It's good to see it looking so well taken of. I wonder if they keep flowers in the back window as I did?"

"Our driveway, Mom," he said softly.

"What?" she asked sharply. "Tobias Seth Clamons, what did you do?"

"I used one of my GI benefits and bought our home back," he replied. "It's just the right size. We can plant flowers next spring. Here, let me open the door."

"You did what!" she exclaimed. "Son, you need your money and you didn't need to go in debt for me."

"Didn't go in debt, Mom," he replied. "Liam and I had it. Our little place was on sale, a little in need of love and repair, and I got a really good deal. That teacher who bought it years ago had moved into town and it was just sitting here empty so I made an offer and he took it. Some friends and I fixed it up. Let's go on in and light the fire. You remember how you used to sit and sew while I read by the fire?"

"Fire?" she exclaimed. He let them in, went over to the fireplace that his friends had left ready to light and set it blazing. The house smelled of tuna noodle casserole and coffee. The fire blazed up and settled down. "Those young men at the house, those friends? This is what you meant by moving day?"

He stood up, smiled and nodded. "No worries, Mom. Just look it over. See if it isn't what you have always wanted. But let's take your sewing things into your sewing room first. We'll eat after you've had a little explore. I'm sleeping upstairs."

"What? Sewing room?" she exclaimed.

"Remember the old study?" He opened the door to a side room off the kitchen. Along one side, under the window, was the sewing machine. Fabric filled shelves lined one side, and a long table the other, with a quilt pin-up board behind the table for layout.

"Oh, my Lord!" his mother breathed. "I don't know what to say! This fabric isn't all mine? And is that my old sewing machine? Really? It can't be! It got sold in the auction when we lost everything."

"It is. My friend Kevin is a whiz with computers, and he looked up the auction and who bought what. He found the present owners and Matthew went to see them. I got it off him and I took it to the sewing machine shop and it's all ready to go. "

She sat down in the chair by the machine and ran her hand along the top. She put her feet on the treadle and gently pushed. "Oh, my soul! I made so many shirts and so many quilts." Looking up, she smiled. "I know I can finish another prize-winning quilt now. I can sew them with my machine, and it will speed it up considerably. I can quilt with this machine, too, you remember?"

"I do. But right now, I'm going to go set the table. You just wander around and be sure we got everything put where you want it to be. I can rearrange the stuff you want to be rearranged. Don't you try to move the furniture. It's your home now, Mom. You rearrange and adjust it to your heart's content and don't worry about a landlord anymore. This is yours and mine and we'll be happy here."

Chapter 3

Two weeks later, Sheriff Erick Black listened to the angry voice at the other end of the line. "Yes, it's outrageous and I'll send the deputy out soon as he returns. Yes, we'll get to the bottom of it. Thom, yes, we'll figure this out. I'll call you as soon as I learn anything." He hung up.

Deputy Malcolm walked in. "What is it?"

"You need to get over to the hobby store. Appears someone broke in last night and stole some merchandise."

"OK, I was headed that way anyhow. I'm going to take a lunch break afterward, OK?"

"Sounds good. You be in the same place?"

Malcolm nodded. "Same bench in the park. I'll stop by the diner and pick up the usual and relax a bit."

His boss answered. "I have these idiot forms to fill out from the state. They want to know how many major crimes we've had this quarter. Does shoplifting count? Or maybe jaywalking?" He shook his head. "Been quiet most of the summer except for some touristy blundering around. Now we have another break-in. We might have to start carrying pistols. Well, find out what's gone." He grumbled and settled in, turning back to the pile of official forms and the deputy left.

On arriving at Thom's Hobbies, he found Thom and Suzanne both present. Suzanne was looking at a fabric square.

"You are not going to believe this Brad," Suzanne reported. "Someone got in the back door, stole an RC truck, and left this. It's called Arkansas Traveler. I looked it up to be certain."

"Excuse me? You are handling evidence why?"

"Oh, sorry, didn't think of that." Brad slid the block into an evidence bag.

Brad sighed. "Let's start at the beginning. When did you discover the truck gone?"

Thom answered, "I opened up shop at 10, as usual. I went around and discovered the back door open, which is odd since I never really unlock it except to bring in new stock. It doesn't look forced."

"Let's go start there. Show me the door."

Thom led the officer to the back of the shop to a door, now closed.

"How did you find it?"

"Well, it was open, about this far," Thom unlocked and opened the back door so it was ajar around eighteen inches. "I looked around back here and didn't see anything wrong, so I relocked it, and went out front. That's when I saw the display over here had been tampered with. Four of the boxes were opened but nothing was taken out of them. I counted and realized the Master Gravedigger Express that was on the top was not there. I got a ladder and in its place is where I found this quilt square. I went over and showed the wife and she told me the pattern. It's weird because this RC company is from Arkansas."

"So, someone would have to know quilts and RC cars to do this?" asked Deputy Brad. "Do you have a picture of what's lost?"

"Sure do. Right over here on this poster. It's signed and everything by the operator of the actual Gravedigger truck. It's really popular with the teens. The truck was a limited edition and it costs retail $599.00. I've looked all over the store but didn't find it, so it's been taken. Isn't something valued over $500 a felony?"

"It's felony theft and then we need to add breaking and entering as well, but it didn't look broken, almost like whoever it was had a key."

"I don't have a key to the back. I always lock it from inside and then I go out the front door. When I want in, I go in from the front." He looked a little sheepish.

"Fire marshal know that?" commented Brad.

"Actually, yes, he does. There is another way in and out, I have three access doors to the outside. See right here is the big arch door into my sister-in-law's fiber shop, hi ladies!" he called out to the women in the shop who waved, looked at him and the deputy curiously, and went back to finding just the right yarn. "There's the front door, there's the back door which is openable in case of fire, and then there's the basement."

"Basement?"

"Yes, right here, open this door here and go down the steps, it's steep, watch your step. I store the inventory down here, that hum is the dehumidifier, and see, all the shelves are pretty – well, what the ding dong heck is going on!" he cried.

In front of him, several sets of shelves were knocked awry, their merchandise scattered all over. The door to the outside was standing open, and going out, the deputy saw truck tracks in the dirt. He looked and saw that the tie-up post for the Amish horses that was behind the store had been broken over. Turning around, he saw a graffiti patchwork square, a match to the fabric he held in his hand, spray-painted on the back wall in bright blue, green, and white.

"I think we need to add criminal mischief to the charges," the deputy said quietly. "And this door's been jimmied so I think we know how the shop was opened. Can you go through everything and give me an itemized list of what's damaged, what's missing, its value and maybe a picture? I need to send out an alert on all the places that deal with pawned toys, I think. By the way, did they get to the cash register?"

"I keep it empty at night, and I was just so frustrated when I found the truck gone, I mean it took me a backorder and three months to get that truck in here and now look at this mess!" He went over and looked at the door. "Door doesn't seem jimmied..." He reached for the knob but Brad stopped him. "Let the lab guys shut it," he said softly. "Just leave it all be till the guys get here."

A visibly upset Thom led the way back upstairs. "I'll just call Miriam's brother and see if he can come in to help a few hours to get this mess fixed. I'll need to close the store for a while, blast it, this is Tuesday and the Old Guys Aeromodelers RC club come to talk models with me, buy parts and hold their meeting." He led the way over to the check-out counter. The cash register looked untouched. It was unplugged but appeared to still be in working order.

"Thom, don't touch anything yet. Let me get the guys over here from the county to dust for fingerprints. This is just unreal. And now that you've touched the square, we may need to fingerprint you both."

"No need," said Suzanne. "We've been training to be foster parents and had our BCI check two weeks ago – it ought to be on file wherever they keep those things."

Brad nodded. "Let me just call the county. Close the store, keep anyone out from the other stores, and just wait. And let's do a walk through-all your stores open to each other like this makes it like a little mall, and they could have harmed something else and no one has noticed."

"Miriam's brother will be coming in to pick her up at 4, but she was going to stay over for the quilt club, so he can help you clean it all up tonight, honey," Suzanne said, hugging her husband.

"Thom, I am so sorry." said his brother in law Mike who walked over from his museum store. "Looks like we've got a destructive crackpot in town." He shook his head. Brad nodded in agreement and then continued, "Lock the front door, watch for the county lab guys. Once they've done the fingerprint stuff, you can start doing the inventory and cleaning up. Be sure to itemize a list of anything broken or stolen. I'm so sorry this happened. We all need to tighten up security."

Brad walked out and waited as the family locked up. He got into the car and radioed in, explaining to the Sheriff and requesting the lab. A few minutes later, he was told they'd be here in forty-five minutes.

He let the family know, phoned in to tell the Sheriff and left the store.

Chapter 4

Brad drove over to the Getalong Cafe and got his usual lunch, a salad, tuna fish sandwich, black coffee, a lemon filled donut they kept back just for him, a bottle of cold water, and a bag of homemade chocolate chip cookies.

He drove to the park. Getting out, he walked over to the bench overlooking the back of the school and watched the kids come out by classes. Noontime, the children came out; one group to work on their garden beds, one group to eat at the picnic tables, one group to run and play on the new playground equipment in the park. The littles, kindergarten through second graders, were eating, the third and fourth graders were gardening, the fifth and sixth graders were in the park for the first twenty minutes, then they all rotated until it was time to go back into class. "Old Amos Mosby is surely good with those kids, teaching them gardening. They look great. Wonder who'll come visit today? I guess my son would have been in second grade this year. I miss Ellie so much. Wonder what she would think of Casey? She's a good woman, friendly, always smiling. Has a tough job. Don't know that I could do it."

Just as he was finishing his salad, a boy came up, bringing with him another two kids. "Hey, Gary. Who's this?"

"This is Bill and his little sister Greta. They're new kids. They moved into the old Crosby place. He's in my grade and she's supposed to be with the third graders 'cept she doesn't talk."

"Doesn't talk?"

"Nope, not a word. I was telling Bill he doesn't have to be scared of you. He's sort of afraid of strangers and cops."

"That so? You all need a cookie to hold you until lunch?" Brad reached into his bag and pulled out three large chocolate chip cookies. Holding them out, he saw how the two new kids hung back and watched their new friend Gary take a cookie with enthusiasm before each taking a cookie.

"Thank you, sir," said Bill politely. "Greta says thank you too."

"She really can't talk?"

"She's just shy. She talks at home." Brad smiled at the little girl who ate her cookie slowly and kept her eyes on her shoes. "Ma got us new shoes yesterday for school. You got a nice store here." Bill remarked as he finished up his cookie. "Is it true you come here every day?"

"Pretty much, I do, this same spot," answered the officer. "My wife and I used to eat here at lunch. She was a schoolteacher. She died when a trucker who had one too many bennies trying to stay awake ran over top her little fiesta car. It killed her and my son instantly. That was five years ago, and I still come here. Oh, and I almost always have cookies. The kids know me. You ever have a problem; you can come to me. You ever act like a bully to the littles, you answer to me, got it?"

Bill nodded seriously. He shook hands with the officer. Greta just looked at him with shy, huge, brown eyes and long, thick eyelashes a model would kill for. Gary slapped Bill on the back and said, "Come on, man! Our turn to garden. You're gonna love Mr. Amos."

Brad watched them go. He ate his salad, finished his tuna fish in three bites, drank his coffee, ate his donut. As he ate, three more children came over for cookies and to say hi. One little girl came and sat on the bench a moment.

"Officer Brad, I think there's something bad happening."

"Oh? You want to get a cookie and tell me about it, honey?"

She took the proffered cookie and hesitated. "I heard the fighting going on again over at Sissy's like I told you about before. Sissy has a big bruise on her leg. She showed it to me. She says her big brother is back, and he kicked her last night when he was fighting with his mom."

"Ah," remarked the officer, taking a bite of doughnut. "She's here today?"

"She's afraid to talk to you so I told her I'd talk to you about it. I tried to get her to come over. She's sitting over there."

"I see her. So, her brother Jim's back? OK. I guess I can visit her mom and be sure everything's alright."

"Sissy said he hit her mom and her glasses are broke."

"I see. Anything else?"

She shook her head. "These are good cookies. I got to get back to class."

The officer waited quietly. He mused. *Don't believe Jim has the smarts to pull these two break-ins off, but that he's back is a problem. Let's see, he got sent up for trying to sell pot to minors, as I recall, and criminal trespass and attempted robbery. What was it, six months? Yes, guess it is time for him to be back. I'll just see if his mom has anything to say.*

He heard a soft noise behind him and looked over his shoulder to find Sissy standing there.

"You need a cookie? Got one left." She shook her head. Wordlessly she came and sat down.

"Need water?" She nodded. She'd been playing hard on the swings.

"Heard your brother Jim's back home? Must be glad to see him. He's been gone a long time."

Sissy carefully screwed the cap back on the bottle. "No," she whispered. "I'm not glad he's back. And I don't like that man he brought with him."

"Man?"

"His name is Dave. He's creepy. Ma is keeping me away from them both but last night," she hesitated.

"I heard there was a fight." Brad prodded gently. He offered her a stick of gum.

She nodded as she took it. "Dave kicked me. And he hit my mom. But Mom didn't have any money and she wouldn't give them the keys to our car. She has to have it for her job." She pulled up her pant leg and he saw a boot print bruise on her calf. Brad sighed and shook his head.

"They got no use to treat you like that, Sissy. That must hurt like heck. Did your mom put ice on it?" Officer Brad spoke softly, but he was battling his testosterone as he looked at the small girl.

"It hurts. I can walk on it, and Mom says it's not broken, and she had me put ice on it. He broke her glasses and we taped them together so she could go to work. Jim just stood there yelling and he did nothing. Since Pa's gone, we got none to keep him away."

"You want me to talk to your mother?" he asked.

Sissy looked down. "She won't listen. She's scared. And they're there all the time. I don't want to go to no foster home."

"If I can convince them to leave, you won't have to do any such thing. You sure you don't want this last cookie?" She shook her head. "Amy needs it more. Her kitten died."

"You send her right over, then. Your mom works the afternoon shift, doesn't she?" Sissy nodded. "And you go to Mrs. Richard's house after school till she gets you. I'll go over tomorrow morning and talk to Jim and your mom."

"I wouldn't have said anything but I'm afraid for my mom and me. I don't like that Dave guy. If he was gone, Jim would listen to Mom." Brad nodded. Sissy got up and left.

Shortly, a little girl came over and claimed her cookie and he sympathized about the kitten who had been grey and white and purred a lot but had contacted some cat disease and the vet couldn't save her. She left. Brad checked his watch, sipped his coffee, threw his trash away.

An athletic woman got out of a green Volvo, walked over and sat down. "Out of cookies again, I see," she smiled. "What's a girl gotta do to rate a cookie from you?"

He grinned. "Hi, Casey. How's life?"

"Not bad. Listen, I need you to watch out for something for me? This new family moved in; they came from another county and we think they were trying to skip county and lose their CPS case. Dad's in prison, Mom has an alcohol problem, lots of family secrets, two kids. Maybe she's trying for a new leaf, maybe she's trying to get away from her CPS case, but in Ohio, your case just follows you since we got that state system put in, SACWIS. Her case just transferred to me. I haven't met her yet. I'm going out this afternoon to introduce myself to her. She works at the laundromat. Dad's in for armed robbery. They're in the Crosby place."

"Met the kids, I think, little boy and girl?"

"Sounds about right."

"Greta's real shy, doesn't talk, Bill seems OK. I need to pass on something else." he quickly outlined the problem at Sissy's house.

"Sounds not good." Casey frowned and stole the last bite of his donut.

"I'm doing a well check tomorrow morning. Mom works three to eleven as a nurse's aide. I need to look up the Dave character."

"Keep me posted. Sure you're fresh out of cookies?"

"Yep. You hungry?"

"Nah, just riding your case. You take care, Brad."

She started to get up but Brad cleared his throat and asked, "How's your little girl?"

"Her team just got second in the state. She is some proud of her trophy."

"Second's not bad."

"For a first time run, absolutely not bad. Those kids tumbled their hearts out. Next year, they want to win the cheer championship and go to nationals and with the present coach, they've got a real chance. She about yelled herself hoarse." She paused, got up and smiled at him. "Have to get back at it."

"You free for supper Sunday?" he asked.

"Not on call," she answered. "So, guess that means I'm free. My mini-me is going to her grandma for the weekend so I can catch up on paperwork. By supper, I ought to have it conquered."

"You like Italian?"

"Love it. Carbs are just what I need after a long day of juggling case notes. Wish to goodness they'd get another caseworker hired on. They've been advertising but folks are afraid of what we do."

"It's not easy work," he replied. "About six then?"

"Sounds like a plan." She turned and he watched her walk off briskly, with purpose, back to her Volvo, climbed in, backed out of the parking lot, and headed for her next appointment.

"She's nothing like you, wife," he said to himself. *"But she has a great heart, she's always smiling, she's dedicated to keeping families safe, and I sure am lonesome. I miss you and sonny so much."*

Chapter 5

Brad Malcolm drove out to the old Crosby place and parked a block down from the house. He watched and observed quietly. He saw Sissy's mom come out and get into her car, driving it away. He supposed she was headed in for work early. He wondered where Sissy might be.

Then he saw a couple of young men come out, cussing her out and acting obnoxious. One threw a show after the car as it sped off. Brad quietly walked over and approached them from behind.

"Hot, damn! Can you imagine that bitch? I needed her car! She could have waited and driven us into town so I wouldn't be late for the appointment. She isn't due at work for half an hour," stormed one young man.

"I bet if we burned this place down, she'd cave." replied the other, lighting up a cigarette. "You honestly don't smoke inside?"

"Sissy's got asthma, so no. Don't like to see her get sick. Besides, burn down the house? You crazy man? I live here. No use burning our own nest."

"Well, not all the way. Just enough to scare her. By the way, where's that little sister of yours?"

"Sissy? Probably in her room. Why?"

"I got me an idea to make some money. Won't hurt her none."

"And do I want to know what this idea is?" asked Brad who was leaning against the house, arms folded, listening.

The two men whirled around. Brad smiled. "Morning, Jim. Back from prison, I see. This must be Dave."

"How'd you know I was home?"

"We get notices from the jail when someone from our area is released. You got out two weeks ago. You been holed up here? Don't you have to report to your PO?"

"Mom wouldn't let me drive in to do that," he protested.

"You think your PO knows that? And tell me about your friend."

"You got nothing on me, cop," spat Dave.

"Maybe not now but let me run your name. You meet in jail?"

The two men glanced at each other.

Brad pulled out his phone. "You want I should call your PO and let him know where you are? Have you even checked in?"

"I checked in before I came out and told him I'd have trouble getting in. He lets me phone him," protested Jim.

"So, why'd you need your mom's car? And where is Sissy?"

Just then a green Volvo drove up. It pulled to a stop and Casey got out, smiling, her purse hanging from her shoulder.

"They're kinda old for me to be dealing with, Brad," she said quietly. "Look to be over 18."

"Not them. Sissy," he replied softly. "Now Jim, where's your sister?"

"She don't need your kind, now," he said sullenly. From an upstairs window, there came a shout, and then he heard a thumping noise.

Brad came out from beside the house and looked over the porch to where Sissy had gotten out her window and was on the porch roof. "Sissy, hey wait, honey, what are you doing?"

"Mommy locked me in the room and said I wasn't to come out until she came back or somebody she sent came for me. She didn't want me to be loose near Dave no more on account of he hit me again." She slid to the edge of the porch. "Catch me, Sheriff?" He reached up and she slid back into his arms.

He caught her and said, "Honey, you haven't got any shoes on. What's going on?"

"I only got my school shoes and I'm not allowed to wear them except when I go to school or church or the store."

"I see. So just socks?"

"I got a bunch of socks. I got on two pairs. That church lady gave them to Mom."

He nodded and turned around. "Sissy, this is my friend Casey. She is going to talk to you a bit and I'm going to talk to Dave there and your brother."

"Is she going to take me away?" asked Sissy, looking scared. "Mom won't like that. She says Casey is one of those people who put you in foster homes."

"You got no call to talk to my little sister," began Jim. He was silenced by a poke from his friend.

"No, sweetheart, I don't think you're going anywhere, Sissy," answered Casey smiling. "Can we go sit under that tree over there and talk awhile? Deputy Brad wants to talk to your brother, and they need some privacy – you know, grown-up men type talk. It's really kind of boring. We can talk over there."

Sissy frowned. "Mom will be mad I came out of my room."

"Well, I'll tell her you were obeying a cop, how's that?"

Sissy considered. "Well, Mommy says you have to listen to the police. OK. But I can only go as far as that tree over there."

"I've got a blanket in my car. Help me get it?"

"OK."

Casey went to her car and pulled out an afghan from the back seat and a couple of bottles of water and her briefcase. She and Sissy went to the tree, Casey spread the blanket in the shade and they sat down. "You had breakfast?"

Sissy nodded. "I had cereal. Mommy fed me 'fore she went to work. I have a peanut butter sandwich and water in my room for lunch. Mom said she'd bring pizza home for supper and salad. I like salad."

"I love salad. I haven't got any with me, but I was going to have a granola bar for a snack. You want one?" asked Casey, handing her a bottle of water and offering her a granola bar. Sissy took it. "What grade are you in, Sissy?" she asked.

"I'm in fourth. I like my teacher but it's teacher off service day, so we got no school. This is a good granola bar."

"It's apple cinnamon. It reminds me of when I was a kid and Mom would bake oatmeal cookies and put chopped apple in them. Why is your mom working now? I thought she worked nights."

"She got called in for an extra half-shift, and she couldn't get hold of Mrs. Richards, so she's going to call on her break and see if she'll come to get me. But I got books up in my room and I got a DVD player and some movies, so I'd be OK 'til she came back. I just have to keep the door locked so Dave and Jim can't get to me."

"What would happen if they did?" asked Casey. She had quietly turned on a little recorder.

"Jim got mad and kicked me and see I got this big bruise on my leg. And today when I finished breakfast, I was helping Mom in the kitchen and they came in and started wanting the car and Mom said she had to go to work. And I told Jim to stop bothering Mom and Dave hit me and knocked me down and Mom screamed and told me to go upstairs and there was a lot of yelling. And then Mom went upstairs with the sandwich and the water and told me to lock myself in, she had to go for a while and she left and then the police came and now he's talking to Jim and I have to be able to get back into my room because mom and me don't think they're safe. Jim didn't use to be mean, just stupid. The other guy, that Dave person looks at me funny and it makes me feel, I don't know just weirded out." She seemed to say the above all in a rush. Her eyes teared up. She started to breathe heavily.

"Sissy, do you have an inhaler?" asked Casey.

Sissy nodded. Her face was starting to pink up. "It's up in Mom's room."

"OK, let's you and me go get it and then we'll talk a little more." Taking her hand, Casey walked back to the front door and went in. Jim and the deputy were still talking.

Jim had been watching them. "You are not going to take my little sister," he insisted.

"After I look Dave here up, I would suggest you call your PO and start the walk into town," answered Brad. "It's just three miles to the courthouse and let's see, your appointment is at 1, you ought to make it easy by then."

"I can't leave Sissy here alone."

"You were planning to take the car and do that earlier," replied Brad. He had both men's driver's licenses and was inputting them into the cruiser computer.

"Walk?" scowled Dave. "I'm not walking into town. I'll wait until you come back. I can watch the kid."

"I don't think so," replied Brad.

"Can you give us a ride, sort of unofficial?" asked Jim.

"No, not allowed. Not arresting you for anything so no, not allowed. Besides, the PO will want to get a look at your friend here."

"I got no warrants." snarled Dave.

"Didn't say you did. He's going to want background though. And Sissy will be coming with us to Mrs. Richard's house. Casey has already called her and will take her to the babysitter since you won't be available to babysit."

"Mom's going to kill me," groaned Jim.

"Least of your problems. Why'd you kick your little sister and leave a boot print."

"I didn't do any such thing."

"She's got a boot print. I saw it. They don't occur naturally." Brad said in a flat voice.

"Well, I didn't do it." protested Jim.

"Dave then?"

"Don't bring me into this," growled Dave, snuffing out the cigarette with his boot. "I'm just here for a place to stay."

"What are your plans for maybe getting jobs, helping your mom with bills and settling down?" asked Brad. Both men looked at him as if he were talking a foreign language. "You do know that's part of being out, right? You got so many hours of community service and have to find gainful employment?" Jim shook his head.

"Nobody wants to hire somebody just out of jail."

"So, explain that to the PO. Listen, we're going to do some background checks; we're going to speak with the PO and you're going to walk to town. Casey will take Sissy to Mrs. Richards and tell your mom what's going down by phone. I'd suggest you all find another place to stay tonight to give your mom a chance to calm down. I'll be watching you."

Casey came out of the house. Sissy had on her shoes and was carrying her doll. She came over to Jim.

"Jimmy, Casey is taking me to Mrs. Richard's house, and I'll come home with Mom. We talked to Mom on the phone and she knows about it so it's OK. You don't have to stay watch me at all so you and Dave can go play."

Jim knelt by his little sister. "Look, Sissy, I'm sorry about the fight this morning. You have a good time at Mrs. Richards. She used to watch me when I was a kid. Tell Mom I'll be back tomorrow."

"OK." She followed Casey over to the green Volvo and got in, fastened her seat belt and they drove off.

"You trust that broad?" Jim asked Deputy Malcolm.

"Casey? Yeah, she's alright."

"She's social services, right?"

"None of them any good," interjected Dave. "Your sis is in big trouble."

"I don't think so," said the deputy. "I've known Casey a long time and she's a straight shooter. She says they're going to Mrs. Richards, that's where they're going. You two now, don't know where you'll end up. It sure won't be in daycare, I hope. Three meals and a cot isn't all that great. You best lock up your mom's house and get on down the road."

Brad waited until Jim had gone in, gotten a soda, and locked the door. He and Dave headed down the township road, softly arguing, getting louder as they got farther away. He watched them. Dave was trying to make some point and suddenly went over to a field and climbed over the fence.

"Ah, blast it. I should've known. He's a city boy," Brad muttered to himself. Jim was yelling at his friend who tried to cut across a pasture.

He got around fifty yards in when there was a commotion behind him. Bellowing over his territory, a monster longhorn bull came charging across the field. Dave took one look at the creature thundering towards him and tore to the nearest fence, diving over and landing in the ditch as the bull pulled up short and bellowed again.

Brad wandered closer.

"What the devil was that thing?" Dave gasped. "I thought you said cows were nothing to be scared of, man."

"That wasn't a cow, that was a bull. Old Mr. Yarman raises longhorns. Gets good money for the horns once they're butchered."

"It could have killed me."

"Yeah, and you could have hurt my little sister bad kicking her and slapping her this morning. Don't think I'm okay with that," replied Jim.

"You're full of it."

"Least I'm not the one all mucky from ditch diving. There's a safe shortcut to town. You better stay with me if you want to make it."

"You better watch your back."

"Yeah, Yeah, Yeah. That talk may work in prison but out here, it don't amount to much." The men started walking down the road again. The bull whirled around and trotted back to its fence line.

Brad smiled to himself and got into the car.

Chapter 6

"Mom, I'm home. Got a surprise," called Toby.

"Son, I have supper already waiting for you and I'm a little old for surprises." His mother came out of the kitchen with a smile on her face, wiping her hands on her apron. "Although lately, I've been getting quite a few I've been liking. You do too much for me, though."

"Nope, never too old for some extras," he replied, setting his boxes down on the table and hugging her. "Now, have I got about a half-hour before supper?"

"Just about that to wash up and put your things away," she replied.

"Then I have one more thing to bring in from the car and I think, let me see, right here, this wall is where I'll put it."

"Is it a picture?"

"It's got pictures," he said breezily as he went back out and returned with a box. "There. I'll set it all up after we eat. How was the quilting today?"

"I finished the lap quilt and have it stored up and have two blocks done, both copies. I know which ones you can use for your computer shop." She paused, "Now I made macaroni and cheese and hamburgers and salad and I've got warm chocolate chip cookies for dessert."

"My favorite." He leaned over and kissed her cheek.

"You said last night was your favorite."

"When my mom cooks for me, it's my favorite," he smiled.

"Oh, you sweet-talker. Will you say grace for us?" she asked.

"Sure, Mom. Did you know the Amish don't say anything when they pray?"

"They must say it in their hearts."

"Maybe so." He bowed his head. "Heavenly Father, for the food we are about to eat and the hands that prepared it, we are truly grateful. Amen." He looked up.

"Dig in, son. You been working hard. What was it like today?"

"We had a full spate of patients, mom. From an 18-month-old baby to a 76-year-old man and everything in between. Lot of colds and flu this time of year. By the way, have you had your flu shot?"

His mother sighed. "And got a pneumonia shot and a shingles shot and Lord only knows what else. I am sick to tears of needles."

"Goes with the territory of keeping you healthy as we can," he smiled. Visiting, eating, reminiscing, the dinner hour passed pleasantly.

"Now, son, you don't have to clear the table. That fancy new dishwasher you put in does most of the work. Least I can do is carry things to the sink. You have those boxes to attend to," she protested as he got up and picked up his plate.

"For once, Mom, I am going to agree because I really want to get set up in the living room. See you in a few minutes. You enjoy puttering."

He took off for the living room and began to tear open the boxes. Humming to herself, his mother set the kitchen to rights, finishing by sweeping. "Cleaning up my own kitchen is not work at all, it's a pure pleasure," she declared as she came in. "I'm just going to set down here and sew a little while you work." She sat in her rocker and picked up her quilt block. "Why did we need a desk chair?"

"Cause we need a desk."

"Oh," she replied. Thinking to herself, she decided he most likely needed to have a desk for work he was doing. She'd never have needed a desk herself; she seldom wrote letters anymore.

She concentrated on the block, basting carefully so she could treadle it together. Finally, she heard her son get up and start hauling out the cardboard to the back where they burned their trash. A computer sat on the newly put together desk. She eyed it with a wary expression on her face.

"Now, here's the surprise Mom," he said coming back in. He sat down and started typing. A screen came up and suddenly, she saw her sister's face.

"Hello, Toby!" his aunt exclaimed. "You got it up and working! Is your mom there!" Marie was standing behind her son, her hand on his shoulder, gaping at her sister on the screen. He got up and had her sit down.

"Mom, welcome to Skype. You and your sister can talk back and forth from Chicago now. If you set up a time to meet each week, you can talk face to face and never even leave home."

"Honey, is that really you?" gasped his mother.

"Yes, it is. And the nice thing about this is you don't even have to type. We can just talk back and forth like we were there."

"Really? Is it expensive?"

"Doesn't cost a thing," replied her son. "Now, you just enjoy your visit. When you're done, Aunt will close down her side and I'll close down this side. Then I'm going to give you your first computer lesson. Oh, and don't forget to set up a time for you two to get together again." He smiled, patted his mom on the back and went upstairs to his room. An hour later, he had taken a shower, laid out his clothes for the next day, read a couple of chapters and decided to see how his mother was doing. He just got there in time to hear her saying goodbye.

"OK, let me shut it down on this side. Now," he said. "We need to set you up an email account, and a Facebook account, and an Amazon account,"

"Good gracious, what are all those things and why do I need them?"

"Mom, this is the time we live in now. I wish we had had this while I was in the military. Anyway, let' me get you all started. When was your appointment to talk to your sister?"

"We thought maybe next Friday evening about 6?" she asked.

"Excellent. We'll just put that in the calendar, and it will beep to remind you."

"She looked so good. I haven't seen her in years." His mom's eyes misted up. "She said she'd have her grandkids come next time. I never thought I'd see her again this side of the grave. Can I see my brother in Phoenix?"

"I can contact him and see if he has Skype," replied Toby.

"I still can't believe it. It's like something out of one of those old Star Trek movies."

"Well, this is just the start of things I have planned, Mom," he promised. "Life is going to get a lot easier for you now if I have anything to do with it."

Chapter 7

The phone rang. Brad picked it up. "Lyonsville police station, Deputy Brad Malcolm speaking. How can I help you?"

"Brad, this is Franklin Jobbs. You member you sent that boy Jimmy into check-in? Sent him on foot with a guy named Dave?"

"Absolutely. How'd it go? Did he show up?"

"Yep. Ran Dave Ranson aka Dave Smith Aka Dave Lyric; Jim met him in prison and that's a no-no on his parole rules. Also, they had already gotten started into some mischief; got a report they were selling weed to some Amish at one of those rumspringa parties in a barn. Not good. At any rate, Dave is a registered offender, tier two – not supposed to be around kids. Also had not registered a change of address. Since there is a kid at the house they were staying in, he's been shipped back. Jim had the choice of leaving his mom and going into the halfway house in Columbus or sent back for six months for breaking parole. He chose the halfway house. Ought to be quieter up your way now. Thanks for locating and sending them in."

"Thanks for taking care of that. Surprised they went in to talk so easily."

"Well, actually they didn't. They came into town, had lunch at the diner, and someone called in a tip they were there. Not certain who it was, but Mick and I went over and walked them back to the office, ran prints. Anyway, long story short, they tried to bolt, we cuffed them and hauled their asses back here, ran the prints and they're all taken care of. Odd thing, Dave is usually a dresser; he had mud all over his clothes. That's unusual for him." Brad briefly filled him in on the bull incident. After a good laugh on both sides, Brad hung up.

He called Casey. "Casey, problems with Sissy are solved. Brother's been sent back, so has Dave. Just the two of them now, Mom and Sissy, so ought to be safe for the child; there are still some poverty issues but nothing that can't be worked on without a case. What? Yeah, I know you're going to go see her mom this afternoon, so maybe pass on that she needs to get the guys' clothes together and she can drop them off here. And see that she signs up for the Christmas gifts from the local church. It's anonymous and Sissy will have a better Christmas and for sure get the food for a good Christmas dinner. We still on for lunch? Good. Meet you in the park. I'll remember to get extra cookies." He hung up and smiled to himself, then turned back to enter his report.

Fall moved on bringing rains that stripped the trees of leaves. There was a chilly wind that blew around the buildings, sneaking into houses and making normally warm homes seem cooler. Thermostats were turned up all over town. Folks started wearing sweaters and hoodies. People seemed to scurry on the streets, umbrellas at the ready, heads down, hardly looked at each other as they got things done and got back into the warmth of their homes. Kids didn't come out for lunch anymore and the school gardens were shut down for winter. The tourists were all gone and everyone seemed to take a collective sigh and settle in for quieter times.

The lab report came back on the two break-ins in town, but it was inconclusive; both were public places and there were simply too many prints to sort out a suspect. The first frost happened, people cut back their gardens and mulched them in for winter, lawnmowers were cleaned up and set into garages and storage sheds, snow blowers were tuned up and ready, the last green tomatoes were gathered in to ripen in the house, the hanging pots were put away. Christmas decorations were hung around town but not turned on yet.

Miriam and Lydia came into work Tuesday before Thanksgiving with troubled faces. Eli, their brother, dropped them off and went home quickly. They both went into their respective places and greeted their bosses.

After a while, Alyssa started wondering what was wrong. "Lydia, you're so quiet. Are you feeling ill?"

"No, Alyssa. I'm fine."

"Your family OK?"

"They're just fine as well."

"Well, I can tell there's some struggle going on and if we can help at all, you know we will."

Lydia looked off into the distance, considering. "I am worried. It is not our way to go to the Sheriff when something happens, but I feel differently about this."

"This?"

"Miriam and I discussed it on the way here. I talked to the bishop yesterday and he prayed and he thinks it is for the good of all concerned. I am just feeling queasy about it."

"Now you really have me worried. What's going on?"

"Could you go with us over to the Sheriff's office at lunchtime?" Lydia evaded.

"I'll be glad to, but we could just have him come over here. You might be more comfortable."

"I'd not want customers to hear what we need to say."

Alyssa nodded. "We can talk in the break room then. Let me call now. Sooner done, sooner left off our hearts and on someone who can do something about it."

Alyssa called just as Suzanne came over with Miriam. "Alyssa," she started. Alyssa held up one finger and spoke quietly into the phone.

In a short time, Deputy Malcolm was in the store. "Ladies, what can I do for you today? It sounded serious."

Miriam took a deep breath and held out a quilt square. "This was found on Mark Beiler's farm. The fence had been cut and his goats chased out. This was tied to the fence. The goats were caught before they did any real damage, and none were hurt, but why would someone let the goats loose in the first place? That was Sunday afternoon, and it was a church Sunday, so no one was home anywhere. We thought at first it might be youth on rumspringa or scholars being mischievous but all the children were accounted for when it happened. Oh, and earlier you knew that the old treadle machine that Hershberger's bought at auction years ago was taken from the barn? It hadn't been used for a few years since his wife had gotten a new machine a couple of years ago. It's odd to me they should steal such a thing. It was a Singer as I recall, a bit fancier than we were used to, fancy decals of roses and daisies, but it worked well. It was in good shape, in one of those pretty cabinets that close all in on themselves. Still, not worth more than a couple of hundred dollars at the most."

Suzanne looked at the square, done up in red calico, solid green, and white with tiny yellow flowers, all good quality cotton. "I believe the pattern is Broken Rail Fence."

Lydia took a deep breath to speak again, but her boss interjected. "Brad had heard about the sewing machine and I believe there was a square there too."

Lydia nodded and continued, "And then on Monday, Gabriel Hostetler came into town to get some supplies and while he was gone, the new chicken house he was building for his wife burned to the ground. He'd run out of nails and since the wife needed groceries, she gave him a list and he headed into town. She was out working in the garden when she smelled smoke and came to see what was going on, and the frame he'd put up was knocked over already and was burning. She found this quilt square on her front porch. It's Hens and Chickens. It's not an easy block to get right."

"I can see why you made an exception and told us about this," Brad nodded. "Thank you, Danke, for coming to us. I'll go out and talk to both families if you think the bishop won't mind."

"I shan't mind as I am here," came a deep voice. Bishop Byler stood in the doorway of the breakroom. "Wie busht du Height? How are you today, Officer? I came in to see if I could help Miriam and Lydia get through talking to you, but it's evident they have said what they know. This matter is of concern to our community, as it is of yours. Lydia told me there had been other incidents with quilt squares?"

"Indeed there have been, and if I collect many more quilt squares, I'll be able to make up a quilt myself," complained Brad. "Would you mind coming to talk to the families involved with me?"

"I think that would be an excellent idea and one I was going to suggest."

"Then no time like the present. Good day, ladies. We will get to the bottom of this."

As he turned to go, Suzanne said, "Incidentally, Brad, did you notice all the quilt squares are nine inches? All the same, in blending colors. Maybe they are planning a quilt of some sort, I mean all the squares would fit together nicely. And if there is a pattern, perhaps we can head this off? May we have a picture of the quilt blocks left at the crimes? Perhaps I can place them into a known pattern and get some ideas of what might happen next."

"The sheriff has the others, get a picture of these two and then we'll leave. I'll send over pics of the others when we return. And thank you so much for your help." The Bishop got in front of the patrol car with Brad and they drove off to the farms. He radioed in and explained the situation to the Sheriff, who took pictures of the other blocks and sent them over as an email attachment to the quilt shop. Suzanne took the pictures, printed them out, and hung them up on the bulletin board.

Over at the Sheriff's office, he was marking with push pins on his township map where the events had occurred. He put the fabric squares in evidence bags and set the file on his desk in the inbox. He muttered as he studied his map. "No pattern I can see other than quilt squares at each one. We have got to get to the bottom of this. I hope Suzanne sees some pattern; I just don't know enough about sewing. Working at the college, teaching the history of quilts as she does, she ought to come up with something. She has those books she wrote with all those patterns and all. I wonder if these are in her books? I'll have to ask."

Chapter 8

The bishop was quiet as Brad drove the squad car on country roads slowly, avoiding potholes, waving occasionally at folks in buggies. "It's such nice countryside out here," remarked Brad.

"Yah, it is. And up till now, we've had good relations with our neighbors. It troubles me that we are being attacked."

"As it does us."

"I would not have known about the trouble in town had Elijah not brought it up when he was at church. He mentioned it and I checked with his wife, and we realized it must be the same person who damaged your stores that attacked our homes. We just want it to be peaceful again."

"I couldn't agree more," replied Brad. "Here's the Beiler place. Do you want us to go in together, or how would they be most comfortable?"

"They know we are coming," the bishop replied. "Thank you for coming so soon. Here's Jethro Beiler to come out and speak with us."

Brad parked and they got out. By the time they had circled the car, another man had joined Jethro.

"And this is Gabriel Hosteler," introduced Bishop Byler.

Brad nodded and shook hands. "Sorry about your henhouse, Gabriel, and are the goats okay, Jethro?"

"We caught them all. We have 40 head that we milk for market. It was quite a job to get them back in. They like to ruined my wife's flowerbeds. Seems they love late zinnias. Wife had covered them so the frost wouldn't get them and guess they just looked green to the goats."

"What was the extent of damages?" asked Brad. He had his clipboard out and was taking notes.

"We retrieved all our goats, so other than aggravation, not too much damage, but my wife's flower beds we just tilled under. Minor damage, I'd say. We were going to do that shortly anyway. Still, it's the thought someone would be angry enough to do us spiteful harm," replied Jethro.

Gabriel nodded. "And had I had the henhouse done, we'd have lost our flock, but they were in the old henhouse. I lost the costs of some lumber and time. I'd guess a couple hundred in materials is all. I'd have thought it was some sort of accident except for that quilt square tied to the toolbox. I gave it to the bishop and I think he gave it to Lydia to bring in?"

"She did bring both of them to me. Hard to believe a lady who sews so well could be behind this," Brad shook his head. "Of course, I guess a man could make quilts as well. At any rate. I've written down what you've told me and what the ladies said, and if you could just read the statement, add anything you want to, and sign and date the reports, I'd appreciate it. You're sure nothing was stolen?"

"We can't locate that old sewing machine. We bought it quite a few years ago and the ladies used it, but they got a new one from Lehman's' and they retired that one and only used it as an extra machine for when the other women come over for a frolic. It was under a tarp in the barn."

"May I see where?" The men led the way into the barn, to a stall where a tarp lay neatly folded. There were some scuff marks on the floor of the stall but nothing else.

"Did you disturb this in any way since the disappearance? It's not like crooks to fold up tarps neatly."

"This one did," answered Jethro. "We came and found it just as you see it."

"Not quite," came a quiet voice. Mrs. Beiler walked in. "There was a quilt square. I found it and thought it too nice to throw away, so I made it into a potholder. I didn't realize at the time it had to do with a bunch of crimes. I'm not one to waste things, so I made it up and I am sorry. And I know when the machine disappeared. We had a frolic in July and we had it then. My boys brought it back out and we covered it well. We were to have a frolic again in September and it was gone then. So, between July and September, it walked away. It's one of those things you don't notice until you need it. I laundered the potholder so it would be clean for you." She handed him a quilt block that had been neatly made into a potholder. The pattern was a pieced sewing machine done in red, green and ivory.

"Thank you." Brad took the potholder. "So the sewing machine incident happened months before the goats?" Mrs. Beiler nodded and left.

Brad frowned, looking at the stall. "They hit you twice then?"

"Maybe so," Jethro agreed.

Brad put the potholder in an evidence bag. "Thank you for your cooperation. May I take you back to your farm, Gabriel? I'd like to see where the fire happened."

"I walked over, so yah. Bishop, are you coming?"

"Yes, I will ride back into town with Mr. Malcom since my buggy is waiting in town with the wife doing shopping."

At the second farm, there was a pile of neat lumber waiting to be built over the ashes of the old. "We're having a frolic tomorrow to clean up and rebuild," said Gabriel. "Normally wouldn't for such a small building but the community wanted to help so we'll have a new one in place by supper."

"That's marvelous." Brad walked around the ashes, took a couple of pictures with permission, studied the site. He lifted some ashes and smelled them. "Definitely used an accelerant, I'm guessing barbecue starter from the odor. See this streak in the grass? He poured the accelerant from here to there when he had sprayed the uprights and stood back, made sure no one was about and whoosh, one match and it's gone. But why? Do you have anyone angry with you or anything? Someone who might want to get back at you both? It seems a strange prank to play. I mean if it was kids, it wouldn't be done this well." He took an evidence bag from his pocket, scooped up some of the ash and tucked it away. "Where was the quilt patch?"

"It was tied to my toolbox. Right over here by the fence." Gabriel gestured, "Right here. It had a string wrapped around it. It was the blocks made us think they might have something to do with what's happening in town."

"You were right to call and talk it over. And as soon as we know something, we will be getting back with you." Brad and the bishop got back into the squad car. They drove back to town and Bishop Byler met his wife at the grocery. Brad went back to the station, added three patches to the evidence file, and marked the incidents on the map. He took photos of the potholder and sent it to the quilt ladies.

"Let's send the ashes over to the fire chief. He can test them for accelerant," Erick said quietly. "Wonder what this patch is?" The phone rang. "Sheriff Black. How can I help? Hi, Suzanne. It's called Grandma's Sewing Machine? Thanks. We'll add it to the list. Yeah, two patches at Beiler's. I don't get why they got hit twice. Yeah, I agree. Well, if I don't see you before. Have a good Thanksgiving."

"Label this patch Grandma's Sewing Machine – it dates back to the 1950s," he instructed Brad. "So what do we have? Hen and Chicks, Broken Dish, Broken Rail Fence, Arkansas Traveler, Grandma's Sewing Machine. They have anything in common?"

"All patchwork," started Brad. "All the same fabric. Suzanne said it was all 50's patterns so far. Expertly done but left at the sites of minor crimes. However, they are getting more serious – a broken window, a stolen RC toy, and a ransacked shop, a stolen antique sewing machine, 40 goats let out, burnt down henhouse; money-wise they're getting more expensive, I think." He looked at the map.

"They're sort of scattered all over. The two farms are up here. The two stores are close to each other, the same block. They all happened in the last four weeks or so. Jim and his friend are gone so not suspects. Suzanne says she thinks she knows most the quilters in town and none of them seem like someone who could do this stuff. I don't see much for leads." Erick shook his head. "I'm switching the on-call phone over to my place now. You have a good night."

"Casey and I are having Italian at Ricci's."

"You really ought to get serious about that lady. She's a good one."

"I know. We're getting to know each other."

"Keep thinking about it. Keep her away from that monster dog of yours."

"She likes animals."

"Most ladies do not want something the size of a calf in the living room. Trust me on this." Erick said, shaking his head. "See you tomorrow."

Chapter 9

At four-thirty Tuesday afternoon, the Thanksgiving program at the school was well attended by pretty much everyone in the town, as usual: parents and grandparents, cousins and local officials. The high school auditorium was decked out in festive banners, baskets of flowers and a large pile of food the children had collected for the food pantry drive lined up in the front of the stage. Local agencies had tables in the back of the hall, displaying their accomplishments from the last year, asking for donations, suggesting ways to help. For a small town, there was an impressive showing of local agencies.

The elementary grades performed a short play on gratitude, pilgrims and a few token Indians carrying toy stuffed deer hanging between two long thick sticks. The chorus sang Thanksgiving songs almost on key and almost in the same rhythm as the piano. Parents stood up at odd times to take photos of their kids. No one seemed to mind.

In the meantime, the middle and high school kids' science fair was held in the gym. During the program, the projects were judged; after answering questions, each child was dismissed to join their family in the elementary program which caused a sort of constant juggling of seats over in the auditorium. The winners were announced after the elementary program completed, ribbons handed out to winners and everyone progressed over to see the projects. Kids stood by their displays nervously explaining why baking soda made cakes rise, why breeding white mice with grey mice made mixed mice, why plants without light didn't grow. At six-thirty, everyone went to the cafeteria for hot cocoa, coffee, and cookies made by the high school economics class. School break officially started at its conclusion and everyone went home with visions of Thanksgiving dinner.

During the evening, the weather got colder. The sheriff and his deputy were settling into the slower pace of fall with the tourists mostly gone, the winter coming in, kids in school (except for Thanksgiving break), and waiting for Christmas. The official town decorations were lit the Friday after the program, glowing snowflake arrays on the light posts downtown, the store windows set up to the general theme of family and the holidays. First Church set out their beautiful life-size nativity in their yard; hand-painted, life-sized plaster figurines that had been used by the community for well over fifty years, donated by one of the founding fathers of the church three generations ago and imported from Germany, well-loved and such a part of the season that townspeople said they didn't feel Christmassy until it appeared. No one quite remembered when a half-circle ring of spruce trees had been planted to protect the nativity, but they were over forty feet high and quite full, with mature holly bushes planted under them, sporting red berries this time of year. The nativity sat back in under the trees, sheltered from the weather, lit up by spotlights at night. The site was a popular one with people who wanted to meditate, show their children or grandchildren, take pictures next to a glittering wise man, or just relax and enjoy. A couple of concrete benches were placed strategically where in summer they overlooked an annual flowerbed, and at Christmas, the nativity. Older folks could be seen after church just sitting and admiring the quiet.

First Church's nativity went up promptly the day after Thanksgiving. The spruce trees' branches had lights attached to them first, with some bulbs here and there and a star carefully put in the center tree, not quite at the top but high enough to be seen easily. "I'll need a taller ladder next year," grumbled the star-setting deacon.

"Or maybe we can borrow a cherry picker," answered the man steadying the long extension ladder. "You 'bout done? Careful now."

"There, that has it. Even if we get some wind before Christmas it ought to stay straight. Bound to be at least one good storm before then. Here, get the end of the wire attached to the power box down there on the ground." The older man climbed down the ladder. When he was down, he flipped the test switch. The star lit up with the fifty bulbs that were attached to the frame. "Looks great. They'll be able to see that all the way over on the highway. High school kids ought to be able to see it over at the school." He turned them back off. "Now let's get the drills and screw the stable together. Have you got the bag of screws?"

The three deacons who erected the set said doing so kept them from having to go with their wives to the Black Friday sales at the mall, but the care they took in assembling the statues, touching up little spots with paint, being sure the fake jewels on the wise men were stuck on well, all accounted for, none missing, shined up and sparkling, the gold in the wiseman's box repainted with gold paint and then adding glitter to it before it dried, the spotlight just so to give the best advantage at night, showed their actual commitment to the task. Sunday afternoon, the congregation always dedicated the nativity to service with a musical program for the community, first in the church at five, then a processional to the side garden, everyone carrying lighted candles, and after a prayer, the lights were turned on in the blue spruce and everyone, holding lit candles, sang Silent Night, Mrs. Reeves did her yearly solo, O Holy Night, the pastor prayed and then all recessed to the church basement for cider and homemade donuts. The homemade donuts were famously good, warm and crusty and soft inside, sprinkled with cinnamon sugar or iced in maple, made hot in the kitchen as people devoured them, standing around, laughing, talking, enjoying the night. Everyone in town came to the program, even the home church folks. It was a tradition. And around seven-thirty, the local stores opened and Christmas shopping officially started in the town. They might have all gone to the mall twenty miles away for Black Friday shopping, but after the nativity service, shopping in town was brisk, enjoyable and friendly. The merchants put out refreshments, there was Christmas music over the loudspeakers, carolers form the church wandered around in groups, there was even a man roasting chestnuts that were gifted to everyone.

As far as the rest of the town decorations, the city workers had been working for two weeks previous to Thanksgiving getting the town decorated. In St. Edwards Park, lights were put on all the smaller trees, large plastic bulbs hung on the branches just out of reach of mischief, a Santa's house set up, (with Sam Beiler, a volunteer fireman who wore a full white beard all year long-acting the part of Santa every Friday afternoon and Saturday evening and for a couple of hours after school) and the town fountain was covered in lights. After the yearly Christmas walk the first Friday in December, the town held a community tree lighting service. After an afternoon walking through the town and seeing the decorations, eating cookies and chestnuts, popcorn and candy set out by the merchants, everyone met in the park to sing Christmas songs that had been published in their weekly newspaper. The town council each year chose a child to flip the switch but this year, it was decided that the entire cheerleading squad from the seventh grade would do the honors. Their appearance had not been announced in general, and the local almost-state-champions came suddenly out of the back of the parked school bus, in their uniforms, shaking their pompoms, yelling,

"Hey hey, get outta the way!
Santa's landing his sled today
Ho, Ho, please don't go,
Kiss me under the mistletoe!
Smack a rack
Smack a rack
Siz Boom Bah
Santa's coming
Rah, Rah, Rah!"

They dashed up, cartwheeling, somersaulting, ending with a pyramid, rolled out of it, gave the last yell and then the head cheerleader bussed the town manager who was standing uneasily by the podium, then hugged the minister, and finally flipped the switch, turning on all the lights in the park. Just as all blinked on, it softly started to snow, just a few flakes as if choreographed right into the show, and everyone applauded.

Finally, the city fire truck arrived, lights flashing, Santa riding in the cab along with Matt Armstrong. The grand old man got out of the truck, called out "Ho Ho Ho, Merry Christmas," and Sam/Santa walked over to the Santa house and went in to greet all the waiting kids and hand out candy canes. He turned on a small space heater, took a swig of his coffee mug and greeted the first child.

He had an elf, really Jane Long, who was short and thin with a pixie haircut she'd dyed green for the occasion, wearing a set of red tights, bell earrings, pointed shiny red sequined shoes, and a green skirt, standing by with a tablet, supposedly adding requests to Santa's list. Her green and red Amazon parrot Max sat on her shoulder and tried to steal candy, but settled on making wisecracks and eating almonds, scattering their shells on the ground. He entranced the children with his "Hello, Johnny" and "Make a wish, honey bunch" declarations.

Just when it felt like it couldn't get more perfect, the pastor's wife Lizbeth pulled up, jumped out of a green Prius and ran over to the Sheriff.

"Erick, the church has been vandalized. You've got to come quick."

Those around heard what she said and spread the word, people dashed to their cars; the Sheriff and deputy got into the squad car and drove the short distance to the church to be met by the head deacon.

"It's the nativity, Sheriff," he was almost crying. "Our beautiful nativity. Just come."

Leading them away from the parking lot to the grove of trees, he showed the Sheriff and deputy as well as the council what had happened, as a crowd from the town joined them.

The wooden nativity shelter and the manger had been broken to pieces. The life-size plaster figurines had been knocked over, chipped, parts broken off. One of the shepherds had been beheaded and his head was found sitting on top of one of the ironwork fence posts in the fence that surrounded the cemetery. People scattered around, finding pieces, bringing them to lay together, trying to be sure all the pieces were together. It was as silent as a funeral as folks gathered and laid out the figurine parts. Some people were crying, several were furious, several were just standing still as if in shock. Deputy Malcolm studied the scene, then went over to one of the trees behind the nativity, pulling something off the branch. He took it to the Sheriff. "Looky here, Erick," he said quietly. "Wonder what this one means?"

In his hand was a quilt square. He waved at Thom and Suzanne and they came over. She looked up at the sheriff and said, "That pattern is called

Crown of Thorns," she said softly. "It's normally in Easter quilts for obvious reasons. Why would it be here at the nativity, and what on earth is this person thinking?"

The sheriff shook his head. "I just wish I knew."

Casey, who had attended with Brad, was on her phone. She was nodding. "Thank you, Cylinda. I appreciate it."

She came over. "Look, might not be my place, Pastor, but I know a family of artists. I'm pretty sure they could help repair this. At least some of it. I've asked them to come over in the morning. I suspect this is a crime scene right now, but if you could meet them at 9 tomorrow, they'll be bringing their pickup truck and good chance if we have all the pieces they can repair it and we can put this back up in time for the baby Jesus to be added."

The Pastor shook his head. "Who could have so much hate in them to do something like this? And during Advent?"

The deacon grimaced. "And to fix it has got to be expensive. And professional artists?"

"Don't be so sure," replied Casey. "Just be here at 9 tomorrow and I will be too and maybe something good can come out of this."

"Well, I can build us another stable," said one man. "I'll just take some measurements. "And I can build us a manger as well." He pulled out a tape measure and, with a friend, wrote down measurements. "We've needed to replace the old wooden one anyway, and we can build a stronger one. 'Twon't be so easy to break up if they try again."

"I can bring in new hay bales," said a farmer. "No problem. Got a barn full. Lord's been with us on hay this year. I'll have it here at Sunday service."

"Leave the spotlight to me," said the town handyman. "If it's not fixable, I'll replace it. And I can repair the control box and lights as well. Me and the boys will be here in the morning."

"Several of the glass ornaments are broken," said Matt Armstrong. "And the lights as well. I have some just that style at the hardware and we can bring them over in the morning. If you deacons can meet us all, we can have it all ready for the figures when they come back."

"Thank you so much, everyone," the Pastor was standing next to his wife. "This nativity has been such a tradition here at the church, but maybe this will be a means of bringing us all closer together."

Casey interjected. "Let's see if we can have it all back before next Sunday. Thanks, everyone. Brad, how long will it be a crime scene?"

"We'll finish up and take down the tape by nine tomorrow," he promised. "Nothing else to see folks, get back and let us work. If we locate more pieces, we'll put them up here. Right now, you're all tramping on any evidence." People moved off, muttering and talking as the snow fell quietly on the ground.

Chapter 10

Casey and her daughter Anne were in Distinguished Shoes talking to the owner, Betsy Bayou, trying to decide on some winter boots for Anne.

"I like Mugs, Mom," Anne said. "But the coach says they don't support my feet well enough. He wants us to have something that does that. But these are so pretty! And feel how soft."

"I have an idea," said Betsy's husband, Bill, coming in from the back room. "We just got some boots in that might make you and coach both happy. What size are you? Nine? OK, be right back," he called as he disappeared behind a curtain.

"I thought he had all the boots on display already," apologized Betty. "I wonder what came in? Even I can't keep up with it and I work here."

Bill came back with five shoeboxes stacked in his arms. "These are from a company in Canada, and they're marvelous." He set the boxes down and opened the top one. "This one is a calf-high fringe boot; it has sheepskin lining so it's warm; the soles are thicker, with arch supports built-in and the bottom sole is ridged for more secure walking. And this one is leather embroidered with morning glories all along the front zipper and around." He opened the other three boxes. "This one is black and embroidered with red roses. This one is navy blue with white fur all over the top and a foxtail hanging out the back. And this one is a higher topped boot, laces up the front and fringed with beadwork. They are simply so pretty and well made, I had to get them in. There's a tribe that makes them up in Canada and they're durable and nicely designed, and will keep your feet warm. There's just enough heel to make them pretty, but lots of ankle and arch support. They are a really good value."

"Are they expensive?" asked Casey. "We are on a budget."

"Less than half the Mugs she looked at earlier. I've got a teenager too, remember?" he smiled. "They'll last better than what you'd find at big department stores. Like I said, an Indian tribe makes them and they're trying hard to get noticed here in the states."

The next few minutes were spent with Anne trying on all five pairs, walking in them, making up her mind, and finally settling on the rose embroidered ones as most comfortable. Casey studied the boots for a minute and tried on the dark brown ones with morning glories. "They are comfortable," she sighed. "And I need boots too, I think. I think I need them with morning glories."

"Tell you what," said Betsy, "How about we do a buy first one, get second one half off sale? We're supposed to do that next week anyway and might as well start a day early."

"Really?" asked Casey, "Don't think I can beat that. So, we can treat ourselves a bit early for the holiday."

As they were paying for their purchases, Brad walked in. "Hello, pretty ladies," he greeted. "You two got time for a hot chocolate? I just got off duty and I feel the yen for some good chocolate with maybe whipped cream on top and a warm brownie on the side while talking to two pretty ladies in a warm place. Wind was nasty on my walkabouts."

"That sounds divine. But we have Christmas shopping to get done." Casey smiled as she held up the shoe store bag. She kissed Brad on the cheek while Anne studiously looked another way and rolled her eyes.

"Well, that sounds like fun too," he said. "How about chocolate and then shopping?"

"What do you think, Anne?" asked her mom. "This was supposed to be girl's day out."

"I think it sounds like fun. I could do with some chocolate and he can distract you while I choose your present," she grinned. "Besides, we need a package carrier."

As they made their way back to the Getalong Café, with a cold breeze blowing in their faces but feeling perfectly Christmas-like, they stopped at Casey's car to drop off their boots and continued, window shopping as they walked, to the next shop.

The afternoon passed pleasantly as they made their way to all the little shops, finding just the right things for this or that person on their list, with Anne secretly giving Brad ideas on stuff for her mom, and he doing most the package carrying. Finally, around six all the stores began to close, and they made their way back to the cars.

"Hey, what the heck!" exclaimed Anne. "Mom, look at the tires!"

"What on earth!" exclaimed Casey. "Brad, somebody yes, they slashed them, the air wasn't just let out and blast it! I just bought tires this fall and of course, it's all four of them and look at that, at the car over here and this one and this one, Brad, there must be six or eight cars with their tires slashed in this lot."

"Mom, why is there a quilt square stuck in our tire?" exclaimed Anne as she stood up. "It was shoved in the hubcap."

"Let me have that," said Brad grimly. "Casey, look around and see if there are any other squares, if there are, don't touch them. Just look around and be careful. Anne, you sit in the car. The perp may still be in the area. Let me call this in. And have you got triple-A, Casey?"

"I do and am calling right now."

"I got a feeling a lot of people will be."

"Any idea what this quilt patch is?" he asked her when she put the phone away.

"I do crochet, not quilts," she admitted. "We'll need to ask Suzanne."

"Let me see if she's still in her shop. We're only the block behind. Sheriff will be here shortly." Francis showed up with her tow truck a few minutes later. She had brought tires and was soon switching new tires for slashed tires on Casey's Volvo, running her credit card through the machine and filling out paperwork for the part AAA would cover.

"Good thing we had these in stock." She surveyed the scene; people angrily talking to the sheriff who was taking pictures, talking to Brad, trying to take statements. "I'm calling Stu and having him bring more tires, let's see, that's a Ford, that's a 16, that's a 15, don't think I've got any of those right now. Man alive, how am I ever going to get these folks on the road tonight?" She looked frustrated as she pulled out her phone.

"Most of them are townsfolk and can walk home from here," said Sherriff Black as he came over. "They aren't real happy about this mess. If there's any out of towners, maybe get to them that have the farthest to go first? And I need all the damaged tires for a day or so."

"You can have them all you want. My recycle truck won't be here for a few days and I generally just stack them in back for them to take. So, when you're done, they'll be heading out to be changed into playground mulch." Francis bustled off, finished Casey's car and went to the next one. Stu showed up with his pickup full of tires. "I called our supplier," he announced. "Got more tires coming tonight, varied sizes. We want to get everyone going safely so please be patient."

"Can't say it's a great way to end a day of Christmas shopping," remarked Casey when her car was done. "I'll see you tomorrow, Brad. I suspect your evening off just got busy."

"Right about that," he said. As she settled into her car and fastened her seat belt, she motioned for him to come closer. He leaned down and she gave him a quick kiss. "Stay warm out there," she murmured. "See you tomorrow?"

"See you at the Getalong at 1 for lunch," he answered. "Gotta go."

The sheriff was talking to Suzanne, who had come over from the back of her shop with Thom.

"You got to be funning me," Thom exclaimed. "Same guy?"

"If it's a guy," answered the Sheriff. "What block is this?"

Suzanne studied it. "Same stitching, similar fabric, and the block is called Wagon Wheel. Does this nut stay up nights trying to think of ways to upset folks?"

Sheriff Black shook his head. "I don't know. You need a picture?"

"Hold it up against Thom's back, there, got it. I'll add this to the others. I don't see a pattern yet but we're working on it."

"It has to be leading up to something," worried Brad.

"Yeah, I know. We just don't know what," agreed the sheriff.

"I sure am glad this isn't happening in tourist season," replied Thom. "Stuff like this gets out it could kill the business."

Chapter 11

Suzanne had the quilt blocks from the incidents spread out on her desk. They matched in color and seemed to match in fabric. She couldn't see any other patterns.

Her sister, Lydia, and Miriam came in.

"We've just completed that new display and thought maybe lunch?" asked Alyssa. "It's so cold and snowy out, no one has come in so it's quiet. Whatcha' doing?"

"These blocks. There's something wrong about this entire mess."

"The fact we've not had another break-in or such nonsense is a good thing, sort of. Nothing else has happened out among your people, right Lydia? You have all been safe?"

"Yes. nothing since the first two."

"It's just odd. Anyway, I know this is the last week you'll be here until our Valentine's day sale," Suzanne looked up from her musings. "With Christmas being Friday, you'll have a good long break at home to just be with your families and relax. I brought some things in for us to celebrate what I hope is going to be a quiet winter."

The ladies all went to the break room where Thom, Alan, and Mike waited. There was a friendly little tabletop tree with some gifts under it, a stack of sandwiches, a small crockpot of hot soup, a plate of little cakes and hot tea. The gifts were exchanged, the food eaten, and after some last-minute things to do in the shops, Alan drove the Amish employees home so their brother Eli would not have to come out in the cold.

While he was gone, and after they'd cleaned up, Thom and Mike went to set their stores to rights before closing, finishing out the books for the day and getting deposits ready, tweaking displays for the last two days of sales before the holiday. Alyssa helped some customers chose yarn gifts, showed a beginning spinner how to thread her wheel and start her spinning. (Her husband had gotten her a lovely traveler spinning wheel, but she wasn't supposed to know about it, so she was taking secret lessons so she could hit the ground running, so to speak, Christmas morning.) She sold several drop spindle sets and knitting kits as last-minute gifts. People were at Suzanne's picking up the quilts they'd had professionally quilted and bound for gifts. She made a few more sales and closed her shop when it began to snow again.

"We're going to have a very white Christmas," remarked her husband. "Wish Alan would get back. He's not had his license very long and back roads are apt to be iffy. Listen, can I have small copies, like thumbprints, of those quilt squares? I have an idea."

"Surely, I can just put them into this newfangled copier we're leasing, one at a time and it makes a thumbprint page of them. It's useful in copying quilt patterns. Just watch." She scanned in each picture, darkened them just a little and hit thumbprint. All of the blocks came back as 2-inch squares about half an inch apart on one sheet.

"Outstanding, and if you, dear wife, would write the names under each one?"

"OK, Let's see, Arkansas Traveler, Broken Dishes, Broken Rail Fence, Crown of Thorns, Wagon Wheel, Hen and Chicks, Grandma's Sewing Machine and I already wrote the places they were found across the top; it's pretty small print now but still legible, I think."

"It's perfect, just like my wife."

"And if you don't mind," came a voice, "May I have one of those sheets?"

"Brad, good grief, man, you nearly gave me a heart attack!" exclaimed Thom.

"Oh, he followed me in," said her son Alan. "Said he had something to show you. And sorry to take so long but the roads are getting bad out there."

"I'm glad you drove slowly. Rather have you back late than hurt." Turning to the deputy, he asked, "What's that, Brad?"

"I took a picture of the map where we have these plotted out to see if it made sense to you." He was holding out his tablet. "The pushpins are the locations so far."

"So far? You're expecting more?"

"Serial criminal not caught has a tendency to keep going," Brad said, his normal smile gone, his mouth a thin slice of seriousness. "So far, it's not anything too big but the value amount is going up of the crimes. Like Ricci's broken window was $250 to fix, your RC car $599, the chicken house frame $300, all those tires! Eight cars had the tires slashed, some of them one or two, a couple all four, so seventeen tires had to be replaced at and total costs of $1900. As I said, the value of the crimes in terms of finances is going up. The worst about it all though is that folks are starting to not feel safe in their hometown. Losing that safe feeling, that's not good." He shook his head. "Thanks for the pictures. You think of anything, you tell me. Oh, and here's that town map you wanted me to bring over."

"Excellent. Does it have the surrounding areas?" Suzanne took the map he held out.

"Not really. But you could get the plot map from the auditor's office for that."

"Good. I'll need to pick that up if they're open tomorrow."

"You folks closing over Christmas break?"

"Christmas is Friday, so closing at noon Thursday, reopening Monday. Several sewing machines are being put under trees that I know of and not a few gift cards, so I want to be open Monday for fabric shoppers. Then closed New Year's Eve and New Year's Day and back to normal winter hours," replied Suzanne.

"I'll keep an eye out then. You have a good holiday."

"You as well, Brad. Thanks for the good work you guys do, and Merry Christmas to you and yours," replied Thom, shaking his hand. "And I do know you'll get to the bottom of this."

"And thanks to all the help you've been, identifying the blocks. If you see a pattern, let us know."

Chapter 12

Friday afternoon, Sheriff Black stuck in two more pushpins with a grimace. "You best go out and check on Yoder's place. The bishop is very worried," he said to Brad. "Matter of fact, let's both go. They're pretty frantic about this. Maybe three sets of eyes will work better."

"Another hit? Did it have a quilt block?"

"Yep. I checked with that book Suzanne loaned me on quilt blocks. It's got all our blocks in so far and Bishop confirmed it's called Flying Geese. Flying Geese! Honestly. That's pretty blatant. And to hit up a widow lady with four kids. That's just mean."

"Well, let's head out," Brad said as he zipped up his jacket and put on his muffler. "You been out today yet? It's cold out there. Have they rounded up most of the geese?"

"Not as of when the bishop was here. Still working on it. Seems like half the Amish neighborhood is out in the bushes today. Any evidence is going to be beaten down by the helpful feet." The two men nodded to the dispatcher, got in the squad car, and left.

They drove the short distance to the neat farm of Eliza Yoder. Eliza's husband had died in a farm accident three years ago and she had been working with her four children to keep her home. Normally, her place was neat, well-tended and quiet. Pulling in, they saw mostly Amish youth beating bushes and herding geese and two men keeping the geese from getting back out of the shed once put in. Other men were preparing to repair the door. They wanted the sheriff to see the damage on the door before they rehung it, so they stood talking or doing other chores for the widow. Eliza stood on her back porch, hands on her hips, lips in a straight line, looking exasperated.

"Morning, Mrs. Yoder. Quite the mess here. Have you got most of your stock back?" As the sheriff talked, Brad studied the shed door, took pictures, studied it and took some notes then nodded to the men to rehang it.

"Looks like they tore off the door, no signs of blood or anything but they yanked it off its hinges and sprung them," he reported to his boss. "Due to all the geese collectors, any chance of a shoe print's pretty much gone. I don't see anything to dust. Inside appears he knocked over some feeders and waterers in chasing out the geese. Must have made a terrible hullaballoo. Why didn't anyone hear it?"

"We were staying at my Mamm's for the night," replied Mrs. Yoder. "She's been feeling a little poorly and we went over to stay and do her chores. We settled our stock in, banked the fire and headed over. When we got back this morning to take care of things, the geese were everywhere. The porch is all covered in droppings that froze to the floor, but the ladies will help me clean it. We still haven't caught them all. We put out grain and called on our neighbors and everyone's helping us. It's our way."

"How many geese did you have?"

"We had three hundred and two," her teenage son replied promptly. "We had orders for three hundred, and they were to be shipped today for butchering and delivering to the folks who ordered them for Christmas and New Year's. The same processor contracted with us for seven hundred fifty and they'd picked up the other half already to process. The truck will be here shortly and they'll not be happy that we don't have full count and aren't ready for them. We sort of hoped you could give us an excuse?"

"Excuse?" asked Brad.

"Mr. Sam's was here last week to look over the flock and drop off the cages to pack them all in and we don't want him thinking we are shorting him on purpose. He's been good to us." replied the young man. "He ordered seven hundred fifty for over the holidays, and he's picked half already. This was supposed to be the last and the money was to pay our taxes. He was bringing a check to us."

"I can give you a copy of the report to show him, and I guess just get as many as you possibly can back," replied Brad. "Wish I could do more. Do you have the quilt square?"

"Mamm has it."

Mrs. Yoder took it out of a pocket. "This was pinned to the door," she said. "It's very well made and really quite pretty."

The Sheriff took it. He and Brad examined it. "It's a puzzle alright. Is there any way we could help with the geese?"

"Nay, we have enough helpers. We hope to get as many as possible in by the time the truck comes. I don't know how many short we'll be. No one is counting but everyone's praying. We've got quite a few but we need every one of them for the order. Many came back to the house themselves, looking for the grain and sweet hay inside. Not much forage out this time of year. I'm hoping dogs or coyotes didn't get some of them."

"I sure hope you find them all. Looks like those kinner have a couple more." Brad nodded towards the yard where two boys carried two large squawking geese, struggling a little but pleased to have captured them. A man ran over to help them put them in the shed.

"We've not been paid for them, so Mr. Sam's will mostly be dealing with angry customers." Mrs. Yoder spoke quietly. "I just don't know why someone would do such a thing. I can't think of any I might have angered."

"Beyond me what makes some people's minds work," commented Sheriff Black. "I sincerely doubt you did anything to deserve this. Thank you for contacting us. We'll keep adding pieces of information and eventually we'll find a solution. If anyone else is hit, let us know." The Bishop nodded.

Mrs. Yoder spoke to her son. "We've got to start putting what we have in pens, son," she told her boy. "Get the men to start putting them five to a pen, like Mr. Sam's wants, and to stack them as we usually do. The loose ones aren't going to be easy to catch once we start but the truck will be here any time and we'll go with what we have." She looked up as three teens came up, each holding a squawking goose to toss into the shed.

"Yes, Mamm," he said. He called out to his brothers and the men to help him, and soon they were making short work of packing up the geese, stacking the pens for transport.

"Let us know the shortage, would you?" asked the Sheriff. "I need it for my report."

"I will do that," she replied. "I hope it's not too much." Her forehead wrinkled as she considered. "We had just enough for taxes with this sale."

The Sheriff and Brad drove back to the town. "What the hell?" blurted Brad as they drove past the houses and onto Main Street. The sheriff slowed down.

Somehow, while they were gone on one call, someone had managed to get into town and graffiti almost every store window with Christmas snow glitter spray. Up and down, both sides of the street, wavy lines of white shiny foamy stuff, ending in spray paint on the sides of the buildings and across the window fronts, had appeared as if by magic in the three hours they had been gone. Angry shop owners were walking outside, looking at the messes. That it had happened in broad daylight and no one noticing during the height of shopping was amazing. It had also infuriated the townspeople who were walking around, taking selfies, posting pictures, and arguing about it.

"They sprayed benches with something sticky," declared Alan from his father's store. "I don't know what it is so I'm putting out signs to not sit down. How hard is it to get frozen glitter off windows?"

"I'm more worried about the paint on the bricks and siding," replied his father. "At least none of it appears to be profanity or threats, just, well, odd stuff."

"It's all slogans," declared David Hershberger. "Stuff like bah humbug, the next is best, wait until New Year's . . . On my store, he painted a quilt square?"

"Really?" declared the Sheriff. "I want a picture of that."

Brad sputtered. "We weren't gone three hours this morning out at Yoder's and he or she did all this at that time? Did anyone see anything?"

"He could have started before we left," replied Thom. "Does anyone actually check their sidewalls every day? Some could have been done last night and he just finished it up while you were gone. You left pretty early."

"We left at seven-thirty and it's ten-thirty now, so yeah, not many about, if he had done some the night before, and then before the shops all opened this morning finished the fronts. Who discovered this first? And hey, Bill, I need to get pictures of it all before you start clean-up." The man with the bucket sat it down and stood with his arms folded across his chest, a frown on his face.

"The entire internet will know about it before we can clean it up," replied Thom. "is there any way we can stop people from posting this?"

"Fraid not," replied Brad. "Now who saw it first?"

Pastor Malachi came over. "Friends, I've made a call to a professional group I know that does this sort of clean up. They're good. We used them a couple of years ago when those teens got a little rowdy and painted our sign. They aren't expensive and maybe if they came, their team could take care of it all and it could get done quicker and be back to normal sooner."

The shop owners had closed their shops and were standing in the middle of the sidewalk fussing like wet hens. Shoppers were continuing to take pictures and Brad had a sinking feeling this was not going to be over soon.

Sheriff Black came back to Brad after checking out David's store. "Same square as at the farm, Talking Geese. Same colors, similar pattern, just six feet across."

"Wow," said Brad. "That's impressive. I've got pics of most everything, I think. Did you notice the street signs are all painted over as well? And the stop signs all say 'why' on them. And does anyone know who saw it first?"

"We either have a gang moving in or one hyperactive crazy," the sheriff declared. "Let's get these pictures over and add the locations to our map."

"They pretty much hit everyone on Main street," chimed in Mike.

"Did they get any side streets?" asked Brad.

"No calls about that. I'm going to drive around and check it out, then I'll head back to the station," replied Brad.

"I'm going to go plot this on the map." replied the Sheriff. "See what else we have got."

"I think we need to close town down for the rest of the day and get the cleaners going," said the town manager. "You all in agreement?"

The shop owners looked at each other and then Liam Clamons, the pharmacist replied. "We have two shopping days left till Christmas and we are not shutting down. I have folks who need prescriptions and I can't simply close due to some paint. In fact, Marti's clinic and the drug store are staying open later. There's a lot of colds and such going around and we can't close. Cleaners can work around us and I, for one am going to run a special sale, maybe call it the Prank Sale. I am not being shut down by some weird person who thinks he can control our town." The shop owners all agreed, went back to their shops, and the crowd dispersed into stores to shop. Later, the shop owners said it was their best shopping day since Black Friday.

Two children came up to the thoroughly frustrated deputy.

"Hi, guys." he sighed.

"Mr. Cop, I think we got something you need." said one little boy solemnly. "We saw a man and he was painting with this and he threw it in the trash, and we fetched it to you. I asked him what he was doing, and he had a face mask on and was all bundled and he said he was decorating for the stores. They needed snow and he made snow for them. Then he walked off."

They held out a homemade spray can holder. It held three cans at a time, lined up and when you pressed down the button on the middle can, all three can buttons depressed.

"You saw him first? I mean, actually saw him doing this? Thanks so much for your help. You didn't see his face?"

The children shook their heads. "He had one of those ski masks things on. He threw it in the garbage can back by the grocery," said the other child. "We couldn't reach the other cans. We thought it might be cool to have but we could only reach this and when we saw how mad everyone was, we sort of waited until they went back inside and we came to see you."

"Why don't you show me when he tossed this?" asked Brad. "Hop in my car."

"Really? We get to ride in the cop car?" asked one of the boys. "Can we run the siren and the lights?"

"Not this time. Might scare folks. Let's go undercover." He stopped inside the station and gave the device to the sheriff, who carefully put it in a large evidence bag. He drove the children to the can in question and Brad pulled out five more cans of artificial snow and glitter and put them in another bag. He took the children's names and addresses, reminded them to let him know if they thought of anything else. He presented them with official toy deputy badges. One child brightened and blurted out, "Oh, he was driving a car like the preacher's wife drives. You know that ugly orange one?"

"You mean the orange Volkswagen?" The children nodded and ran off to tell their friends about helping with the investigation. Brad looked for tracks or other help but there were too many other tracks. He drove over to the preacher's house, but the pumpkin bug was sitting in the driveway, still snow-covered from last night, and had not been driven out that morning. Brad drove back to the station, checking side streets on the way.

"Nothing anywhere but Main Street. However, over at the bank, on the back, is the nearest thing to a threat. Someone sprayed, "Quilts won't keep the dead warm." He showed a picture of the graffiti to his boss.

"Print it all out and let's add it to the map, along with all the other graffiti." The Sheriff replied. "There has got to be a pattern. And we'll send the cans to the lab for evidence but I'm betting they wore gloves."

Chapter 13

Miriam and her family drove to church on Sabbath. It was a sunny winter day, with the snow sparkling, the air frozen, trees crackling in the ice. They drove along at a safe clip, the children exclaiming when they saw cardinals in the bushes.

"God is decorating for Christmas with those birds," observed Miriam to her husband.

He nodded. "His Creation is beautiful. I love the peace of winter."

"And tomorrow night is the school Christmas program. And it will be good to see the scholars do their parts. I need to make cookies tomorrow for the program."

They pulled into the Beiler's farm. A couple of boys took their horse to the barn and put their carriage in the lineup along the front. As soon as they got inside, they knew something was wrong. There were troubled looks on people's faces, no one was smiling, and there were whispered conversations here and there. It was much too solemn, not the joyful Sabbath get together that usually occurred.

"What is it?" Miriam asked her own mamm, who was in the kitchen with other women. They seemed nervous as they set the food on counters, warmed the soup, doing their normal preparation with few comments.

"It appears that sometime over the week, there has been more mischief. The Bishop went into town and reported it to the Sheriff already. Someone yesterday went over to Yoder's farm and broke off the door to the poultry house and chased out all the geese. You know they were raising them for sale and were supposed to be delivering them yesterday to the processor. People want them for Christmas and for New Years'. They went all over trying to capture them back. They had over three hundred of them in the goose shed waiting for pick up and I don't know how many they were able to recover yesterday before the processor truck came. I know the sheriff went out already. Widow Yoder isn't here yet today."

"The last I heard," remarked one of the ladies joining them, "Seventy are still missing. It is a great blow to her; she was depending on the income from the sale of the geese to help her with her January tax bills."

"And the oddest thing," said Grandma, "They found a Flying Geese square pinned to the door, or some say tied to a fence and others on her back porch. The sheriff has it now. He thinks it is the same person that has been attacking both us and the English."

"Flying Geese? How odd," Miriam shook her head. "And the others as well."

"Church is starting. Let's get seated," urged Lydia. "We can talk of this another time."

Miriam nodded. She thought to herself as she joined her sister on the married mother's row, "It just occurred to me that the farms that were struck are on the four corners of the town. I wonder if that's a pattern? I'd best tell Suzanne come Monday."

Chapter 14

Christmas morning, Miriam was cooking breakfast when her husband Enoch came up behind her and put his hands around her waist, "Vrolijk kerstfeest, lieverd (Merry Christmas, beloved)," he murmured with a smile.

She patted his hands and continued stirring the scrambled eggs. "And to you mei mann, now don't confuse me or we'll never get the meal on."

"Course you will. In fifteen years, you've not missed a breakfast, not even while carrying our kinner," he smiled as he kissed her. "You were considerate enough to not go into labor until I was fed all three times." She laughed and shook her spatula at him.

He seated himself as she set the skillet of eggs on the table, beside the already full basket of warm biscuits, bowl of gravy, platter of bacon, jams, honey, and butter on the table.

Her children came in from differing directions.

"You washed up, ya?" she asked her son, Micah.

"Yah, Mamm," he said, sniffing at the good smells.

"Mary, Betsy, take your places. How are the chickens?"

"I put the eggs in the pantry, Mamm," replied the oldest daughter, age nine. "That old red hen didn't peck us today. I held her back and Betsy grabbed the eggs quick. We got ten today from the hens."

"Gut! I need them for the Christmas cookies I want to make after breakfast." The family bowed their heads in silent prayer for a few moments. Then Enoch cleared his throat and began handing the biscuits around.

"After we have breakfasted, and since the stock is all cared for, I would like us to meet in the living room for a few moments before we head to our daily tasks."

The children looked up.

Mamm smiled at them. "It is Christmas, children," she smiled. "I have a few little things to share and then this afternoon we will spend quietly home here, just relaxing."

Daed smiled at his family. "It has been a good year, and you all did so well at the program at school. This being Micah's last year as a scholar, it was a milestone for us. Next year, he will be home here, and he will help me. Miriam, have you anything special planned for right after breakfast?"

"Just the living room?" she said with raised eyebrows.

"Well, if I am not mistaken, I hear something coming through the back door."

There was a knock. Miriam went to open it and laughed out loud. "David Hostetler! Welcome and what is that, oh my! Enoch! Are you behind this?"

The children scrambled to the door. David stood there with a large box which he sat down. "Merry Christmas to you all," he smiled. "Our bitch had puppies a while ago and yer Daed contacted me about one of them," he smiled. "This little one is a female, and she has no name and she needs a good home with children who will train her and take good care of her. Is there such a place here?"

"Oh, yes!" exclaimed Mary. "Ever since our old dog died last summer, we've wanted a new puppy."

"Well, golden retrievers are good family dogs," smiled David. "Now I promised my Anne I would be home quickly. I have two more deliveries to make before my breakfast. Have a Merry Christmas." He put his gloves back on and left.

The children were beside themselves petting and loving on the puppy. Daed smiled and then announced. "I have a good place in the barn set up for her already: she'll be a fine farm dog. Let's take her out and then we can get back to our breakfast. Mamm worked hard on it and I'd not like it to get cold." He carried the puppy out to the barn where there was a feed bowl, a water dish, and a warm stall filled with straw and a blanket waiting. The children gave it one last pet and were brought back inside.

"Won't he be cold?" asked Betsy.

"I think not. He and his family are outdoor dogs and used to barns. He might be lonesome, but I understand most the pups are being delivered this morning to new homes." answered Daed. After a few last pats, the family trooped back inside, hearing the puppy whining a bit behind them from the stall.

After breakfast, they all gathered in the living room. After the family reading, Mamm handed out small gifts to the children; new gloves for each one, <u>Peterson's Field Guide to Birds</u> for Micah who loved birds; a coloring book and new crayons to Betsy, some plain pillowcases that had been stamped for embroidery and colored thread and a hoop to Mary.

Enoch smiled at his wife and brought out a beautiful bluebird house he had made for her. She, in turn, gave him a new shirt she had made for him and new gloves.

"Now let's just leave our gifts here for this afternoon after lunch," directed Miriam. "We've some kitchen things to be done, and the men have some barn things to do, and after lunch, we will take some time to just sit and enjoy."

"It's supposed to snow some more this afternoon," remarked her husband. "Sitting in a warm room and reading the afternoon away sits well with me. I've been saving the *Budget* all week. I can hang your bluebird house before I start reading if you like."

"It would be good to have it where I can see it. Maybe by the clotheslines? And reading the afternoon away, that sounds nice. I need to get started on dinner first."

"May we go to the barn?" asked the children as they finished gift giving.

Glancing at Mamm, Daed nodded and they all scampered out.

Christmas passed without incident, as did Saturday.

Chapter 15

Casey and Brad looked at the map in the sheriff's office.

"You guys are supposed to be out to dinner. You going out New Years?" asked Erick.

"Just studying a minute. We're heading out shortly," answered Brad.

Casey smiled. "I'm on call New Year's week, so no, most likely not out but we might be together a bit. Tonight, we'll be together for a while and most likely will go eat somewhere."

"Annie's having a sleepover at Casey's house. I'm helping," he grinned. "So's my dog."

"You're taking that big galoot Rufus?"

"His name's not Rufus. You know that," laughed Brad. "And he's not really all that big."

"Didn't you say he was a cross between a Great Dane, a mastiff, and an Irish Wolfhound?"

"Yeah. He's sort of tall, but he's a sweetie. And the whole house will be filled with seventh and eighth-grade cheerleaders. He'll be scarfing up dropped Fritos and pizza bones and perfectly happy."

"What if someone phones you on the on-call line, Casey?"

"My mom will be there as well," smiled Casey. "Let's hope it's all quiet, but honestly, three adults for eight girls ought to be fine."

"Well, Brad and I have our beepers too," said the Sheriff. "State troopers are manning the roads for drunks, so it ought to be pretty quiet. You could always call in the law if they get unruly." She laughed.

"Seems to have calmed down a little after the Christmas holiday." she smiled.

"It sure was good of those artists to fix the nativity at cost. They did such a good job you couldn't tell where the original cracks and gouges had been. Nice bunch of people," remarked the Sheriff. "Real nice ceremony they put on installing the nativity back into service and adding baby Jesus Christmas Eve. The wife enjoyed it a bunch. Well, you best be getting on. I'll hold down the fort tonight. Casey, you make this man treat you like a lady."

"He always does," she smiled, taking Brad's hand. They walked outside.

"We going to noodle night at the Getalong?" she asked as they got into Brad's little Cooper.

"Nope. We're driving out of town to really get away from all our neighbors. Did you hear about that new restaurant over in Byersville?

Mexican? Thought we'd head over there. I have an evening off work and by golly, I am going to be off work."

"Sounds like fun. I haven't had a good taco in ages. And it's close enough I can get back if I have to."

They drove and chatted, arrived on time for their reservations, had a lovely meal and got up to leave. "It sure feels good to be on a date and not wondering if someone is going to tell Mom," Casey said as they walked back to the car. "I love our small town but sometimes it's like everyone knows everyone's business."

"I know what you mean. I don't like to let anyone down."

"Let them down?"

"This whole town wants these incidents fixed, the bad guy found and we are doing what we can but it's just not to the level we can call in the big guys, so to speak, and as much as we go over everything, it just isn't making much sense to us."

"Well, you aren't the only one working on it. Did you see the map over at Thom's?"

"Map?"

"He has a big map of the county and the town set up and he sort of drew out from there the streets and such. He has all the quilt squares pinned like you guys have the incidents pinned, to the map. He and the fiber ladies are trying to solve it too."

"I wonder if they've come up with anything I haven't?"

"Don't know. Sure is a pretty night. Look at those stars."

"You know, it's cold enough and if we got away from the city lights, would be dark enough I bet you could see the northern lights."

"This far south?"

"It's happened."

"What do you have in mind?"

"Put old coop into super low and driving around on back roads with my lady friend."

"Are you sure there's a chance of seeing the aurora?"

"Can it hurt to try?"

She laughed. "Long as I'm home by eleven. I need to be sure my munchkin is in bed and Mom as well."

"We have two hours. Let's mosey."

They left town at nine, drove mainly towards home with some side excursions that took them deeper into the country. At a few points, they pulled into field pull outs to get out and look at the stars, ostensibly looking for signs of the northern lights. With some kisses, hugs, and cuddling, they finally made their way back home.

"Your chariot, I'll have you know, is fifteen minutes early," remarked Brad as he pulled up to the house.

"Good thing." smiled Casey. "Driving around with a handsome lawman can go to a girl's head real fast."

"Driving around with the prettiest woman in town is just distracted driving. Probably against the law and we ought both be arrested," he smiled as he put his arm around her shoulders. "You could share my cell."

"You think Annie is watching?" she asked.

"Naw, I think your mom is. Annie would be grossed out by two old people sparking."

Casey laughed and turned her face to his as he gently kissed her. He held her a moment, they kissed again. "I could certainly get used to having that to come home to," he murmured.

"We might have to convince Rufus."

"His name is not Rufus," protested Brad as he kissed her neck. "And he likes you."

"I don't know, he can look me right in the eye when he stands in front of me."

"OK, so he's the size of a pony instead of a normal dog. He can't help it if he grew sort of a lot. He honestly wasn't that big a puppy . . . well, I guess he was. Had feet the size of an oil pan."

"Why did you name him Rufus?"

"His name is not Rufus. His name is Ruckus because when I used to leave him as a pup, he got all hysterical and I had to have him puppysat so the neighbors wouldn't think he was in trouble. His voice is deep like a pipe organ and it carries. His full name is Rutherford Ruckus Malcolm."

"Three names?"

"He's a big dog, one name didn't quite seem to work for him."

"Rutherford?"

"After a law firm that's famous for civil rights cases. Good people. I was thinking of going to law school, then decided I liked keeping law better than interpreting the law." He kissed her again.

"I really do have to get inside."

"Uh-hum," he muttered. "And I need to go home and get to bed. I have to be on first shift at 7."

"I'll be glad when we can kiss and stay together," she said. "Just one more hug. Gotta keep me warm all night," she sighed as she snuggled.

"Your mom got a date set?"

"Mom? Don't you mean me?"

"She doesn't like me and I gotta get her involved in planning to calm that down."

"No, she wanted me to marry a college professor after Matthew died. I just didn't see a point to it. I couldn't understand a thing he said. I like you."

"How about in spring?"

"Spring?"

"For the wedding?" She considered for a minute. "Maybe late May? If I put in for time off now it actually might be granted by then. Our HR is sort of slow. But it sounds lovely. Let me work on that idea. I really have to go in." They kissed again, and for good measure once more when in the distance, a siren went off, loud, insistent, almost as piercing as a tornado siren.

"What is that?" she asked in alarm.

"That's the bank's alarm. Somebody is trying to get into the bank."

"I'm taking that as a good night! Love you. Get going." She hopped out of the car and dashed up to her house, turned and waved as he sped out of the driveway. She was inserting her key in the lock when the door opened.

"You ran away from him?" demanded her mom. "You can't catch a man that way! What is that racket?"

"That, Mama, is the bank security alarm in case you've ever wondered how safe your money is. If it's that loud six blocks away, can you imagine how loud it is inside?"

"So, he had to go and not come in for coffee? I was all ready to hide in the kitchen closet."

"That's Annie's gig, Mom." Casey laughed. "Not sure Brad will ever get over her popping out when he was carrying the coffee to the living room. Lucky no one got burnt."

"That's when I decided we loved him. He didn't make a fuss. He took out his handcuffs and cuffed her. You remember the look on that child's face? Priceless. He's a keeper. And we're looking at end of May for the wedding. That gives me five months to pull a wedding together. Annie in bed?"

"Five months? I can't pull a wedding together in five months!" protested her mom.

"If I do the planning, it's doable. You can help but it's going to be low key. I already talked to Brad about that. He wants it to be at the park during recess so all the kids can come."

"You have got to be joking? Really?"

"Not exactly. We'll talk later. Right now, I want to get to bed. Got to get up at five. Hope that siren gets shut off soon."

Chapter 16

Brad met his boss at the front door of the bank which appeared to still be locked. Alex Drummel, the bank president and CFO arrived and immediately unlocked the door for them. No one tried to talk over the alarm. Flashing, blinking, pulsing like a disco ball gone temporarily out of sync with the music, the alert light made Brad feel disoriented; the alarm matched the light, strident, like a tornado siren next to a house, getting louder as you got farther into the bank. Shaking off their sensory disorientation, Brad and Erick went in first, guns drawn, and their mouths dropped open at what they saw hanging on the safe.

Alex went over to the alarm and turned it off and turned the normal bank lights on. It was eerie and Brad could feel the quiet when the alarm stopped, as though an echo in his head still remained of the sound. Erick felt his heartbeat stop thudding as normal surroundings appeared. Brad shook his head, steadying himself as he stared at the vault.

Draped over the vault was a giant spidery yarn bomb; the pattern was crocheted skulls, like something a goth kid would make to wear to concerts. The colors were greens, cream, and shiny burgundy. The eyes were glistening red sequins.

"That has to be eight feet across, like a spider web made out of skulls. And sparkly eyes on the skulls? Weird touch," blurted Brad. "I have never seen anything like that."

"Get pictures. If he didn't open the vault how did he trigger the alarm?" asked Erick.

"Our system is state of the art," replied Mr. Drummel. "Once the alarm is set, there are three little laser sensors here, here and here, and all you need to do to trigger it is to break the light. I suspect they did trigger it hanging that whatever-it-is afghan thing." Frowning, he went over to the safe and looked at the afghan. "Looks like it's being held on by magnets, big ceramic ones. We don't have a night security guard since we put in the system, so whoever did this had to know that when Jim goes home at 11, the bank would be empty. The bank vault is supposed to be non-magnetic. How did they hang this thing and is it booby-trapped?"

Brad looked around, "I think I see where the nutcase we are dealing with got in. I'll gather evidence." He took pictures and checked angles, studying the scene. Sheriff Black went with the bank president to check the rest of the bank; teller stations, desks, offices.

"No teller drawers were bothered, nor anything else. But I found this on my desk." Mr. Drummel handed the sheriff a quilt square.

Erick took it, looked at it without comment and put it in an evidence bag.

"I don't see evidence they did anything but wake up the entire county and hang that thing." Brad reentered the front lobby. "There is no sign they had to break in. It appears they were hiding when the bank closed. You know those nice lockers you put in for the employees? The empty one on the end was open. From the looks of it, they got into it, pulled it closed and waited. Had to have been a smallish kind of person. Where's your security cameras?"

"Over here." He led the officers to the security closet. He typed in a code and the computer screen pulsed back. The camera feed flipped slowly, from the lobby, to the halls, to the offices, to the vault, back and forth.

"No footage of the employee room?"

"No. We had to choose the most likely place a robber would break-in, so we chose the doorways and lobby and offices. I didn't think my employees might not be trustworthy so nothing in the employee room."

"The hall in front of the employee break room? Is that covered?"

"Yes, it is, let me see," he ran it back. They watched as sped-up film images seemed to show employees zip in and then out on breaks or lunch. Finally, towards the end of the day, all the employees seemed to go in and come out.

"Check out time. The time clock is in the breakroom. I'm going to go frame by frame and see if I don't recognize someone. We only have fifteen employees and I know them all. Now the day security man is checking in and turning off the alarm, there's Mavis, Sandy, Susan, Marlie, Ed," he watched as each employee went in, came out with their coats and hats, smiling to each other leaving.

Then as they watched, a blurred ghost went into the employee room.

"Someone's tampered with the feed," declared the bank president. "I don't recognize that one and they don't come back out." Later in the images, they saw the night security person go in, come out.

"That's Jim leaving at 11." They waited. About fifteen minutes later, the door to the employee breakroom opened and the same shadowy, blurred figure came out and walked down to the elevator and left.

"That's it. That has to be the person," remarked Erick. "We need a copy of this. Maybe folks at state can decipher how it was done and get us a picture."

"Already copying the last week to a thumb drive. There, that's got it." He handed it to Erick. "You have got to catch this low life. He's messing up the peace of this town and endangering us all."

"I agree. Brad, let's take down the afghan and do a thorough sweep to be sure our bogeyman isn't still here and then Alex if you can reset and relock after us?" It took them until one-thirty to go over the building, then Alex reset the alarm as they left.

They both went back to the station to find their voice mail line flooded. "I'm suspecting that's half the town calling to find out about the siren," sighed Erick.

Brad was leafing through the book they'd been given. "This is called Robbing Peter to Pay Paul," he announced. "Page 53."

"It figures," sighed his boss. "Let's mark it, add it to the pile."

The fire truck siren went off and the truck flew past the station. "Looks like we're not the only ones busy tonight," remarked Erick. His phone rang. "Lyonsville Station, Sheriff Erick Black speaking. Really? I'll send Brad over."

"What?"

"We've had another attack. Must have been during the bank alarm. Go join our fellow first responders over at the Getalong Cafe."

The fire was pretty well out by the time he arrived. Someone had set the grease buckets and the dumpster out back on fire. The back wall had been singed, but a call from a neighbor got the fire department there, just three blocks away, in time to avoid real damage to the building. The owners had just shown up.

"It could have been a lot worse, and we are definitely going to say arson," said the fire chief to Alan Long.

"Who'd want to burn up our cafe?" asked Jane.

"Not certain, but they left this behind." He handed a quilt square to Brad. "That was pinned down a little way along the edge of the roof."

Brad blew out a breath and took it. "Unreal. If you'd not mind faxing over a report when you get it done, Chief?"

"Sure enough. I hope you catch this guy."

Brad took the square back to the station and handed it to Erick.

"Great Creeping Mother of Thyme, another one?" he exploded.

Brad was thumbing through the book. "Looks like Snail's Trail."

"OK, now they are just thumbing their noses at us," growled his boss. "Copy these last two, send them to the ladies."

"Thom's been working on this too," Brad stated.

"I know. I've been giving them quilt square copies and the addresses where they were found. We're all looking for some sort of pattern and it's not happening."

"It's three a.m. Maybe we ought to sleep on it and hit it in the morning?"

"I guess that makes sense. You get the couch; I'll take the cot. Let me set the coffee maker to start up at 8. See you in a few hours, I'll lock up."

"Let me stay. You go home to your family and I'll see you in the morning. I'll sleep on the cot and you go on home. Your wife will be worried," Brad suggested instead.

The sheriff agreed and left. Brad scanned the quilt squares into the computer and sent them as an attachment to the ladies. He locked up the front. He heard a noise in the back of the station and stepped outside the back door to look around, which is the last thing he remembered before waking up, cold, tied up with plastic ties, and lying on a dirt floor.

Chapter 17

Behind the bookstore, lying in the snow, Melody was barely conscious. Looking out his window across the ally, her neighbor saw her and ran out to see if he could help. He rapidly called 9-1-1 when it was evident she was hurt. Sheriff Black called the clinic. Marti Davis, the nurse practitioner, grabbed a bag she kept for emergencies and dashed two blocks down to the bookstore.

The sheriff in the squad car got there just behind Marti, who had sprinted over. She had been on the All-State Girls' track and field team in college and was still in better shape than the sheriff had been even in his younger years at the police academy. She went at once to her patient and cautioned her not to move.

"I'm so cold," Melody complained.

"No doubt. Is the bookstore open? Is there a blanket in there?" asked Marti.

"I don't think so. I was just going in to open for the day and I got hit from behind. I don't think I'm hurt too bad. I get dizzy when I try to sit up."

"I've already called for the ambulance to run you into the ER in Berlin," Marti said. "BP is good, pulse elevated, no blood, but my! You are going to have a goose egg. Your eyes are reactive both sides, so you don't appear to have a severe concussion." She was talking into a small recorder as she ran her examination.

"You say someone hit you from behind?" asked the sheriff. He had brought a blanket from his squad car. Marti took it and tucked it around Melody.

"Didn't say a thing. Just thump and here we are. I'm going to have to change these pants, they're all muddy wet now. And oh!" she swallowed. "I feel like upchucking when I move like that." She swallowed a few times, took some shallow breaths and continued. "It had to happen just as I was opening up," she fussed. "Old Mrs. Myers and her husband come over for a cup of coffee early, to gossip and to read the newspaper every morning and they'll be wondering why the shop isn't open yet." She started to rise and fell back down. "Wow, that does not feel good."

"Just a minute," replied the sheriff. "Let me get something that's under your head." He gently slid his hand under her head, lifted her an inch and pulled out a quilt square. Shaking his head, he pushed his folded muffler under her head for padding on the cold ground.

"Blast it all," he muttered. "This is getting really old."

"That's a log cabin," replied Marti, glancing up as she completed her exam. "Melody, I don't think you are going to have any severe results from this, but I'd feel better if you'd go to the ER. It's a short ride and there are some bad things that a thump on the head can cause. Dizziness and nausea are some of the symptoms of a fractured skull."

"The back door wasn't opened. May I have the key to your shop?" asked the sheriff. "I want to be sure everything is all right in there."

"What earth did they want with me?" Melody said plaintively. "I don't even leave the cash here. Speaking of which, I had my cash bag with me, here it is, still in my purse, and my purse is fine." She opened the bag, glanced in it, zipped it shut. "Nothing out of that. It doesn't look like this was a robbery. Why are they picking on me?"

"No, it wasn't a robbery," replied the Sheriff. "Here's the ambulance. I'll just have a look around and you call me when you get home, all right? I'll just leave the closed sign up. I'll tell the old folks out front you're going to the hospital to be checked out. Then I'll lock up and be sure we go by several times a day to be sure it stays safe."

"Thank you, Sheriff," Melody answered. Marti turned her over to the paramedics and went back to her clinic and a roomful of patients waiting for her with aches and pains, coughs and fevers. Sheriff Black walked around the shop, opened the front door and waved off the folks out front, and locked it up again. He went out the back, looked around for clues, then headed back to the station.

"I wonder where Brad is? The cot hasn't been slept in, so he must not have stayed here. He's always here first thing and he's not checked in." He went over to the radio. "Officer Malcolm, do you copy?" he spoke into the radio and got static. "Brad, do you read?"

Still static. He looked around. There was no sign of Brad anywhere.

Chapter 18

"It's odd Brad hasn't called me," thought Casey as she drove through town after a home visit. "I've left him two messages. He wasn't at the park today, of course, he might not show up as cold as it's been lately. Still, I'll just stop by the station. I did so want him to talk a bit about the wedding."

She pulled up in her little Volvo to the Sheriff's office.

"Have you seen Brad?" demanded Erick.

"I was coming here to try and locate him. Isn't he at work?"

"Station was locked and he wasn't here when I came in; he was supposed to sleep here last night. The cot hasn't been used. I called over to his house and then went over to check. I gave food and water to that monster dog of his and it doesn't look like he went home. Did he mention anything to you about where he might be headed?" Erick questioned. "I've got a bad feeling about this."

"I haven't seen him since last night before all the alarms went off. We were supposed to meet for breakfast today, but he didn't show, he didn't show up to meet me for coffee; he didn't text or anything to cancel and it's not like him to not call or anything. I've been busy so I didn't have time before this to try and locate him. Do you think he's all right?"

"I sure hope so. We need him big time. I'm going to drive around and see if anyone has seen him."

"When was the last time you saw him, Erick?"

"About 3 this morning. He was supposed to stay here overnight. When I got here this morning and he hadn't slept here, I thought he must have gone home after all and slept in by accident. We were late. I was about to go over and check on his place again."

"But he didn't go home?" She seemed a little stunned.

"No. And the door was locked when I got here this morning."

Casey led the way outside. She looked around. "So, the front door was locked this morning. What about the back door?"

The Sheriff led the way to the back door. It was locked. He unlocked it and started to study the area.

Casey pointed to the ground. "Sheriff, does that look like a drag mark to you?"

The sheriff looked at where she was pointing in the snow.

He knelt. "And here's a place a body could have dropped, then someone pulled over here to the alley and it stops. There are blood drops here, not enough to have been shot, more likely hit from behind. Brad's been kidnapped." He stood up, turned around, looked up on the wall and groaned.

Painted on the wall was a quilt square and hung from the overnight box a cloth replica, another quilt block.

Chapter 19

"Miriam, here's the latest quilt squares left on the sites," said Suzanne as she downloaded attachments from the Sheriff.

"I cannot believe someone would do things like this in our town." sputtered Thom. "Look, let's add the latest to my map out back. There has got to be a pattern. We simply cannot be floundering around when someone's been assaulted and someone else kidnapped."

"How many do we have now?" asked Miriam.

"Let's see, we're added the one from Melody's, the one from the bank, the one from the cafe, the one from the Sheriff's office." He pinned up the squares. "Casey is beside herself."

"Ought to be. They're engaged," replied Suzanne. "I hope to heavens he's OK."

"The hits are getting closer together, more vicious, like the person doesn't think they have too much time left," replied Mike as he came to the break room. "And look, I'm not a quilt expert but doesn't it look like one of your quilts when you have it hanging on the wall? Sort of like someone is planning something out?"

"I wonder what the time constraint could be?" Miriam considered. "I can't think of anything happening at this time of year. Everything is usually quiet; it's February, kinner are in school, we don't have anything happening big in town until the end of April when we all have the grand opening at all the stores to welcome in tourist season."

Thom grinned, "Officially it's Founders Day, not a grand opening but sport of like a welcome back. The sidewalk sales and carnival stuff do attract the first tourists of the season officially and have sort of gotten out of hand. I understand they're going to ramp it up a little this year and bring in kid's rides in the park and add a couple more bands and some other things to make it bigger and that is somehow going to make it feel less commercial. At any rate, yeah, you're right, nothing big happening that would make a deadline for this sort of idiocy. Unless the deadline is Founder's Day for some reason. At any rate, the attacks are escalating."

Alyssa came over from her fiber shop. "The log cabin patch, may I see it?"

"Sure, greens, creams and the traditional red chimney." He handed the picture to her, she looked and handed it to Lydia.

Miriam looked over her shoulder and drew a quick breath. "We must talk to the Sheriff, please."

"What's going on?" asked Thom. "Have you figured something out?"

"The middle square of the patch, and this green, yes, please call the Sheriff." Miriam hung the squares back in their places.

Erick came to the front of the shop to find Thom, Mike, Alyssa, and Suzanne looking puzzled and the two Amish sisters very upset.

"Sheriff, this fabric, this one and this one. These two fabrics. I know where they are from," Miriam exclaimed as he came in the door.

"Excuse me?" he asked.

"Last week after church, Mrs. King said she had bought some fabric to make some new clothes, washed it to get the starch out of it and to be sure it was preshrunk. She hung it out on her clothesline. She came back to get it sometime later and found someone had cut a square out of the corner of two pieces. The two pieces stolen were about a fat quarter square in size. They were red and green. She assumed it was kinner playing a prank and we all resolved to discuss such things with our children. But this looks like the burgundy she had and the green she had. And Sheriff, please come to the back of the store. There is this map we have all been working on and I had an idea."

The Amish ladies nearly ran into the storage area. "See, there was no square left at the farm we know of, but the fabric was taken. And if we add this address, look at what is happening. Mike is right, it is a plan."

"I don't see it." growled the Sheriff who was puffing a bit from the chasing through the storeroom to the back.

"The four Amish that were attacked are the four corners of the township map. See? Beiler's, Hostetler's, King's, Yoder's." she paused and pointed as everyone studied the map.

"Their properties surround the town; they own the farms that make a big square," said Lydia in a hushed voice. "And the other places, see how they fit. If we take strips of white fabric, just a second, sister, you think the town map, an inch?"

"Just get the blue binding tape, ¾ inch," Miriam advised. Lydia brought back two packages. "We will pay you for this, Suzanne. If we add 3/4 binding tape for side streets, inch wide for Main street," she opened up the packages and with scissors and pins, cut and pinned in place cloth streets. "And see, with two inches on the county roads surrounding the town, it is all fitting together as a quilt. He is covering us all with quilt squares."

"Quilts within quilts," muttered Suzanne. "And it appears whomever it is hits each place in a zig-zagging pattern. See? First one was us, here, then up a block and other side, here, then Amish corner, then here, here," she pointed out the order by dates.

"Something else; where are those pictures of the graffiti? What do the lines seem to you to be? Leave out the words. Just look at lines." said Lydia.

Suzanne and Allyssa studied. Suzanne suddenly gasped out, "It's the quilting itself. Look, it is not just random lines, it is carefully spaced three lines together, curving up and down here, and two lines zig and zag here on this building. Each building had representations of actual patterns of quilting. This pattern of stitching was popular in the '60s."

"I don't get it," said the sheriff, looking at Thom, who simply raised his eyebrows.

"If you quilted, you'd see it easier. Let's see, I have the normal patterns in a book over here," Suzanne dashed over to her bookcase and pulled out a couple of volumes, finally settling on one and opening a page near the middle.

"See, these were popular quilt patterns in the 60's. Once you complete a quilt top, you have to fasten it to the batting and the bottom; you do that by sewing all three together, usually with a running stitch. We use different patterns of stitching to do that. These look like a form of echo lines, where you run a series of lines out from a piece of applique and sort of make it stand out. And these look like two and three spaced lines, all along the buildings, tying the whole town together. Outstanding! It's really quite amazing."

"Shop owners did not think it was outstanding or amazing," growled the Sheriff. "OK, so what do we have? He's giving us clues that he's making a quilt? What happens when all the parts are assembled?" Thom raised his shoulders in a shrug, Mike shook his head and the men all looked at the excited group of ladies.

"And if what you are saying is right" continued the Sheriff, "then the next hits ought to be either the grocery or the gas station. But what about Brad? I assume his missing means he was kidnapped, but where did they take him? And how does he fit into the quilt?"

"There is an old log cabin on the King's property. They might have him in there," replied Lydia. "It would match; it's located right here, between the two farms; it would fill in this side."

"Might fit. At any rate, I need to go take photos of Mrs. King's fabric. You think the bishop would be available to go out with me?"

"I'm not the bishop but would I do?" came a quiet voice. "I was supposed to meet mein frau and take her to lunch. If she would excuse me, I could ride out with you to King's."

"Lydia? May I borrow Jacob?" asked Erick.

"Ya, the sooner this is solved the better. You go. I hope you find the deputy."

As they left, Miriam spoke in quiet tones to her sister. "Ich verschreck net graad. (I don't frighten easily.)" She shook her head. "I hope Jacob is safe. I hope Brad is safe. My heart is all fluttery feeling."

"Gott verlosst der Seine nicht (God does not abandon His own). I think we're all upset," replied Lydia. Changing the subject, she asked her sister, "This is a special day, ya?"

"It is Jacob's birthday and our fifteenth anniversary. We were going to have a small lunch. I made him a little gift. So many folks have colds and illnesses right now that having a big dinner with family seemed like asking for trouble, but he insisted we do something to commemorate the day and I just don't think this is what he had in mind."

"Well, when he comes back, you go with him to a late lunch," Alyssa smiled. "Fifteen years is a long time."

Thom was still staring at the map. "I am so guilty feeling right now."

"What?"

"As the first hit, we had the least done to us. Poor Melody was physically assaulted, and Long's had their diner set afire and now Brad's kidnapped."

"But we've found a pattern now. Surely the sheriff will be able to figure it out," comforted Suzanne.

He put his arm around his wife's shoulders. "Yes, there is that. Well, I'm back to the shop. We need to get the doors open for people and try to carry on."

"A good idea," agreed Alyssa. "I have just gotten in some pretty skeins from McFarland's."

"And believe it or not, my jobber dropped off fabric for spring already and we need to get some things rearranged."

"Then busy hands make the heart lighter," smiled Lydia. "Let's get going. The sheriff will do his job and we shall do ours. What is that saying you embroidered on that last quilt? Hands to work and hearts to God? I think we all ought to think of that today."

"A Quaker saying from the 1800s," answered her boss joining her. "It's a good one to meditate on."

Chapter 20

"I think this one is your prettiest yet," said the young man. "Mom, you just keep getting better. We can easily sell these for you, Kevin and I."

"Thank you, son," she smiled up from her old treadle machine. "That last fabric you brought me was a pleasure to work with. I just can't see why folks would just want unfinished quilt blocks. Are you sure you don't want me to put them into a lap quilt or something?"

"Oh, no, Mom. These are perfect as they are. Just the right size, all different patterns, no two alike, just perfect. They're selling like hotcakes. One person has bought six of them so far and he wants more."

"Really?" asked his mother. "Well, I never. It's astonishing what tourists will buy, I suppose. Perhaps he's going to put them in a lap quilt himself. Now you've told them I'm not Amish, right? I'd not want them to think something that wasn't so."

"They know they aren't Amish made, Mom. I was careful to just say they came from Amish country." His mother had turned back to the square she was working on, completed the block, cut the thread and stood up to go over to her ironing board, where she trimmed and ironed it flat, adding it to some others already there.

"Mom, would you need one of those small irons without cords you keep at the sewing table so you don't have to keep getting up and down?"

"Oh, lands sake, son, I'm not so weak I can't get up and down three feet to the ironing board!" she exclaimed. "You are just spoiling me something fierce."

"Well, you deserve some spoiling." He watched as his mom squared up the block on her cutting board. It joined two others lying on the table. She studied them, choose one, laid another in a stack of blocks and handed one to him. "There, now I've chosen the one for my quilt I'm making, and this one is a spare, and that one to be sold," she said with satisfaction. "All right then, I have these for you as well. Three more, so you have four. And you're sure they're paying twenty-five dollars each just for a block? I mean, I'm not even signing them or anything."

"Mom, you won prizes at the fair for your quilts and no one pieces like you do. No, don't sign them. People can see they're quality just by looking at them. They're just what I need right now. And here is the hundred dollars from the last batch you made me. Is there anything at all you need?"

"I'm just fine, son. I'm going to go put this in my special savings envelope. I might just buy something extra next time I go into town."

Her son's face took on a thoughtful look. "It's such a long drive into town, Mom. And it's slippery out with the snow and ice. I can bring you what you want or need until the weather is better."

His mother coughed. "You're probably right. It is nasty out. But still, next nice day I am going to town. Oh, I do have a doctor's appointment next week. Remember that. Rain or shine, ice or snow, I have to go in to see Dr. Michaels."

"Thursday, isn't it? And I wouldn't worry. Doctors can be wrong. I know that from working with them. I think you're doing fine."

"I'm not worried. I know my God and I'm ready. I feel fine. I can keep sewing on my old machine here until I'm ready to take it to my bed. I'd like to live before I go though, sort of work on my bucket list."

"What do you mean, live? Is there anything you need?"

"When the weather breaks, if I'm still on this side of the sod, I'd like to go visit my sister in Chicago. I'm saving up all the money from these quilt blocks to go to Chicago. I can take the bus and I can stay at her house and then I can come home to rest. I'd like to be buried in the family plot over by Libreville."

"Mom, don't talk about that."

"I need to, son. I think you haven't accepted what the doctor says. I hope to make it until Easter when all the flowers are out and it's so lovely," she sighed. "And I would like to see Founder's Day. So many pretty flowers. Last time I saw your father and brother was on a Founder's Day. Now, please help me to bed, dear. I am bone-weary. I'll cut out pieces for the next blocks tomorrow. I have enough fabric for four more and that will have to be the end for a little while, I think. I am just weary."

The good son helped his mother to her room. She took off her duster and he helped her climb into bed.

"I don't even have the energy to get dressed anymore, and I feel downright lazy staying in my nightie all day," she complained as she yawned. "That nice nurse lady will be here in a couple of hours to give me my medicine and then another will be back in the morning, so don't you worry. You have a good drive into work; didn't you say you worked tonight? I'm glad I'm helping your online shop get off the ground. Tell me about the shop again, dear. I like to hear about your successes. It does my heart good."

"It's just a little online craft store, Mom. I can open it on your computer and you can see what is sold tomorrow when I get back from work. Come spring when it's warmer, I'll take you to town and you can see the big quilt store, remember the one that used to be there? You used to work part-time there when I was little. It's at least twice the size since those ladies took it over. The one there now is all filled with crafts from local folks, and there are quilts and runners and afghans and birdhouses and wooden toys. They have craft kits people can buy and make up themselves, and it's all very Americana with stars and flags and such. You'd love it. They have a perfect rocking chair by the front window for a person to sit in. Right now, it has a pillow display on it. My online store sort of copies that store in its design and folks like it a lot. The downtown store is just like the one you always wanted to have but couldn't because you had to take care of me."

"That wasn't the reason I didn't get to have a store and you know it. After your father left us, I had to work two jobs and I never could quite save up enough to have a craft store. It wasn't because of you; it was just our circumstances. The bank took our house and we had to come live in that apartment over the store for so long and it was so small and so close. I was glad when you came home after college. Did I ever tell you how thankful I was that you boys were able to buy back our house? I'm so comfortable here. Maybe come spring I can get out and talk to the neighbors if anyone is still here from when we lived here. Is Sophia still in her pink house?"

"Yes, she is. No one's going to move her."

"Then she's the first one I am going to visit. How did you find my old Singer 27 cabinet treadle machine?"

"Kevin searched and found the person who bought it in that awful auction so many years ago, a nice Amish lady she was, and Matthew went out and got it from her son. She hadn't used it in a while, so it was dusty. I was able to get bobbins for it online. Matthew isn't really mad at you mom, he's just confused."

"I've sewn many a good quilt on that machine. And clothes for you as well."

"Maybe so, Mom. I'm going to get going. I want to get these posted. You just sew what you feel you can."

"Did it cause problems when I couldn't sew anything in January?"

"No, no, not at all. I just didn't post anything. Things slowed down a little after the holidays, but we're back on track now. These four will do nicely, to get the memoirs project back up and running again. What are their names, Mom?"

"This one is Dove in a Window. I won first place and best in show for this pattern back when you were a baby. And this one is Bowtie, then Crossed Roads and this one's called Amish Star."

"Thanks, Mom." He wrote down the names on his pad, then he leaned over and kissed his mother. "I'll see you in the morning when I get back from work. You do what you can as you can and I'll get them used. You'll get your Chicago trip come spring if you still want to go."

"Oh, I will want to go," she smiled and snuggled down under her covers. "Lock up before you go, yes, son? My nurse has a key."

"I will. Don't worry."

Chapter 21

Brad tested his bindings. He certainly was tied, but haphazardly, as if by a child, the knots easy to untie. He heard voices outside.

"There are footprints out here by the old cabin," remarked one. "Might be so we find something?"

"I sure hope so." The door was tried and opened. Brad lay quietly until he saw who was there. "Erick! You are a sight for this man's eyes!" he called.

"Brad, you OK?" demanded the Sheriff. He stopped, took pictures, and proceeded to untie his partner. "I am so glad to see you."

"Likewise. The last thing I remember is a thunk on the back of the head. Let me guess, there's a quilt square around here somewhere?"

"Log cabin quilt left in town." Sheriff Black spoke into his radio for an ambulance and forensics team.

"Really? Well, that's apropos, I guess." He reached up and rubbed his head. "Ouch. That's going to hurt for a couple of days. You wouldn't have some ice?"

"I'm surprised you weren't frozen. It was cold last night."

"You mean this morning. Wow, can't lift my head too well, sort of dizzy."

"Be still, Brad. Help's coming. And you disappeared yesterday. You must have been out cold longer than you thought. Stay down till the medics get here. You hurt anywhere else?"

"Hands are waking up and feel like pins and needles. I can wiggle my toes. Back is a bit achy. I'm not seeing double or anything, just a little nauseous. And I sure am cold." He paused and went on. "Erick, why would they kidnap me, leave me in an Amish cabin, and then let me go?" He felt at his pockets. "My wallet's still here, tools on belt, yeah, doesn't appear to have been a robbery."

"They didn't let you go, they may be on their way back, but this kidnapping and the assault last night brings this to the level of a federal crime, I think. I'm calling in the state guys."

"I really hate to do that – but wait, last night?"

"They knocked Melody out on her back step at the bookstore, they kidnapped you, no telling what going to happen next. I hate to call in the state guys; most of them are so pushy, but I don't want any deaths."

"Nor do I."

Jacob spoke quietly. He held out a square of fabric. "Sheriff, I don't believe any of our women would leave this here. It is an Amish pattern but no one's been here for months. The women sometimes have frolics out here since it's so shady." He held out the inevitable square.

"It's Amish?"

"It's called Amish Star," he replied. "I remember my wife making one and calling it that. It was different colors than this and we sold it for the fundraiser."

"I think we broke the pattern," said the Sheriff.

"What pattern?" Erick filled him in. "And this farm wasn't on the list of possible next places."

"And I thought the log cabin block was for me?" replied Brad.

"The sheriff's office was on the list," said Erick. "I guess you qualify as the office."

"That's true," replied Brad. "In uniform, I'm the office, just like you."

"OK, if they are going to stay true to pattern, the next incident is going to be at in the park."

"My park?" demanded Brad. "The one with all my schoolkids?"

"Yeah."

"Let me up. I need . . . oh, my." he laid his head back down gingerly.

"You are going nowhere. I am deputizing folks to keep watch on the park. I'll tell the school the kids aren't allowed over to play until whatever is going to happen over there is done."

They could hear the ambulance coming. Soon Brad was loaded up and headed towards the hospital ER.

Jacob was talking to the farm owners in a hushed voice.

"We thought perhaps we would not have any more problems," said the owner of the cabin, Micah.

"It is in Gott's hands," replied Jacob. "Remember at the meeting the bishop exhorted us to have faith and wait and cooperate with the authorities because whoever is doing this is attacking both the People and the Englishers," said Mr. Beiler.

"It is not our way to get involved, but it would be good for it to be over," replied Micah. The other men nodded. "After all, it has been foolishness, dumm, so far. But now they are kidnapping people, an officer no less. What will they do next? How can we be safe?"

"It is in Gott's hands," replied one. The other men nodded.

"True, but we can watch and we can be vigilant, can we not? Here comes the bishop."

Sheriff Black came out of the log cabin as the paramedics carried Brad out. "Jacob, let's go back into town. You need to get to your lunch and your frau, and I need to get to my calls."

"Excuse me, Sheriff," came a voice. He turned to the bishop. "I have something for you. Mrs. Yoder, the younger, went out last night to help her Mamm and found this hooked to her buggy. It frightened her to find it there. The pattern is called Tumbling Blocks. She looked around and had her son come to get the neighbor and he sent his son to get me. We went into her barn and someone had thrown down a bunch of hay bales and straw bales all over. It was a mess, but no real harm done other than some bales breaking open. We all set together and straightened and sorted and fed the loose hay to the horses and cattle. It was simply an aggravation."

"Mrs. Yoder the younger? Where does she live?"

"Their farm is west side of the town line, just between Beiler's and Hostetler's. Her mother is a widow and so is the younger. Her mother had the geese escape? Now the daughter had the hay tumble."

"Thank you. Every bit of evidence we have will help. You said the hay has been cleaned up?"

"It will be shortly. You needn't worry about it, "replied Bishop Beiler.

Chapter 22

Casey sat next to Brad in the ER.

"How'd you find out I was in here?" he asked quietly. "Man, when I move my eyeballs, I get all dizzy."

"I got my ways," she smiled in a somewhat shaky voice. "Seriously, I have a scanner in my car and picked it up. Are you going to be OK?"

"They've done an x-ray, CT scan, blood tests, urine sample, you know the drill. I got hit on the head, tied up a few hours. I suspect I'll get a cold. I feel a little queasy, kinda dizzy, and my head's pounding. The nurse asked me a bunch of inane questions about who the president was and what day it is and asked me to remember three things. They said they could give me some painkiller shortly. I'll be fine. It's not like I was shot in the line or anything." At her face whitening, he realized he'd said the wrong thing, and he took her hand and held it, leaned back and closed his eyes. "Your boss OK with you being here?"

"Boss told me to go. I'd be too distracted to get ready for the court today anyway and the secretary canceled my home visits for the day. Brent said I could take a couple of days off if I needed to; I have enough days built up if I need it. I almost never take time off and I've built up comp time. They'd rather I use it up than them having to pay me for it at time and a half."

A few moments passed. The nurse came in. "The test results all just got to the doctor. He'll be in to speak to you in a few more minutes. Meantime, here's your Tylenol, and Trazodone, a serotonin reuptake inhibitor – you need to sleep this off, and most likely will need some help getting to sleep so this stuff's the safest. We're keeping you overnight."

"Excuse me? It was a thump on the head, not a full-on collision."

"Doctor will talk to you. Now swallow. There, that's good. You lie back and behave yourself. No jumping around."

"Not much chance of that. Those Tylenol are the size of horse tablets," he complained.

"I got the coated ones so they wouldn't be hard to take," she smiled. "Now lean back. Are you his wife?"

"I'm his fiancée."

"I've seen you somewhere," observed the nurse.

"I'm with Children's Services. I've been in here with kids."

"Ah, yes. Counselor, right?"

"Something akin to that; social worker. I'm in ongoing and act as the agency therapist. What room is he going to?"

"Step down unit room three."

"Step down?" gasped Brad. "I didn't have a stroke."

"No, but you could still throw a clot on us and we'd rather have you where you can be gotten to quickly," said a quiet voice from the doorway. The tall man, dressed in white scrubs, was reading a tablet and walked over to the bed. He shook Brad's hand.

"I'm Doctor Michaels. You police types need to wear football helmets. He got you good. Luckily, he did not fracture your skull, but you have a concussion and need rest."

"What about the other lady?"

"Excuse me?"

"Melody Bibby. She was brought in yesterday with a similar injury."

"I can't discuss other patients, however, off the record and only because you're a law officer investigating events in town, I'd say she was thumped about like yourself, but she had a padded hat on so not as much trauma. The sheriff is handling that investigation, so don't worry about it. Now back to you. You've got a level three concussion; you were out cold for a while and may have sustained some injury that wouldn't show on a CT scan, so you will be going to have an MRI in the morning. In the meantime, we're keeping you here and watching to be sure you don't show evidence of a clot or go into a stroke. You've been feeling disoriented, dizzy, your vision has been blurred, right?"

"Sounds about right. But I can sleep at home."

"Surely you can. I suspect you to be released tomorrow unless something shows on the MRI. Is there someone who can assist you once you are home? You're going to need help getting safely to and from the bathroom, for instance, and helping you get meals. Are you still nauseous?"

"A bit. Especially when I move my head."

"Not unexpected. We will get you back on your feet as fast as we can, but really, you got a heck of a lump back there."

"It smarts."

"I have no doubt. They'll refresh your ice bag when you get up to the unit. Now when you go up to the step-down unit, your physician will change from the ER doctors to the hospitalist on duty. Sheriff Black said he'd stop by this afternoon to check on you. However, he knows you're going to be out of commission for probably three to five days, then back on part duty for another three. Your own physician will take over care once you get home. Do you have any questions?"

"No, guess not. Can I have my phone?"

"Once you're out of ER and up to your room. Nurse gave you an SRI to help you relax and sleep and it will serve double duty in helping you relax in the MRI machine first thing in the morning. Noisy bugger, that. Here's transport to take you over." He made sure Brad's wrist band was secure. "Keep track of that. Miss?'

"Casey. I'm his fiancée."

"You might want to take this interlude to make some phone calls, catch some lunch if you need to. He's going to be asleep most likely very soon. He'll be settled into room three in about an hour."

"Thanks." She leaned over and kissed Brad. "I'll be waiting upstairs, Brad. No worries. Take care. Be nice to the nurses."

"Like I'm going to get hurt in a hospital?" he tried to grin at her. The orderlies unlocked his bed and pushed it out of the room. The nurses replaced it with a bed from the hallway and another person was brought in.

"Busy today?" remarked Casey to no one in particular.

"Yes, we are. This is his bag of personals: can you take it with you to his room? Transport should have kept it with him but we're in such a dither. Car crash out on the highway; injured coming in."

"Surely, I can. Thank you for all your help. I believe I will catch some lunch on the way up."

Casey lugged the paper bag with her on her way to the hospital cafeteria. She picked up a tray, balanced the bag, her purse, her briefcase, the tray, and tried to reach food to the tray from the cafeteria display shelves.

"Hey there, Casey, what on earth you doing, girl?" came a cheerful voice. "You're going to need PT services if you keep this sort of thing up. You want salad?"

"Hi, Andy, How's the social work business here?"

"Lots easier than what you're doing," she paused. "Let me set this stuff over on the table right there; no one's going to bother it and get your arms free. You do realize you're surrounded by the PT staff right now? They all go to lunch at 11:30 and the eyes they're giving you for using your body wrong, girl, you don't want to see." Quickly taking the bag, the briefcase and the purse, she sat them at her table.

"Thanks. That was awkward," sighed Casey. "Let's see, salad, roll, a slice of cheese, slice of apple pie."

"Put it on my tab, Sally," she turned to Casey. "My treat this time. You got it last. Now, what brings you here? Another sad case or family?"

"Brad's been hurt in the line. He's getting an MRI."

"That gorgeous hunk of guy is here? In this hospital? Is it bad?"

"He's my fiancée and they say it's not but they're keeping him and doing an MRI tomorrow."

"You're engaged? I didn't know! Let me see that ring. Lordy! Look at that! I've not seen one like that before." The ring was made of white, rose and dark gold twined into a Celtic knot in front, where a diamond was seated in a ring of alternating opal chips, white, fire, black, around the center. It was simple but breathtaking, and the sparkle addicting to watch.

"He designed it himself, and his brother, who is a metalsmith, made it. The gems came from a ring his father had."

"That is one of a kind. He must love you a lot," remarked Andy.

"And I him. Some crank hit him on the back of the head with a blunt object."

"Ouch, blunt force trauma; that is not good. Do they have the guy?"

"Still at large but not for long. Sheriff Black has about had it with the shenanigans in this town." In just a couple of moments she described the quilting criminals and their actions.

"That is so odd. He leaves a quilt square? So appears to me you just need to bring in everyone who makes patchwork, no wait, that's got to be hundreds of ladies, a few men and doubt any of them are young or spry enough to do this stuff."

"Right. I don't like to think of the civil liberties you just broke by making a hobby into a profile," Casey said with lifted eyebrows. "We have to get it narrowed down more."

"You staying with your man?"

"I intend to but need to make some calls. You know, your chef ought to be complimented. This doesn't really taste like cafeteria food."

"See all those young guys over there? Local vocational school has its class here all week apprenticing. Food's been great."

"So it's too much to hope for that the food stays like this?"

"It's like this three times a year; Christmas and once first semester, once second." They both laughed and sipped their coffee.

"Well, listen, I have to get going. I have stuff to do on fourth floor," said Andy. "Want me to keep an eye on Brad?"

"If I'm not there, it'd be appreciated. He's sort of out of it now and maybe doesn't realize it. Don't let any used car salesmen in."

"Got your drift and got it covered."

Andy left, her shoulder bag swinging, Nike shoes blinking. Casey smiled after her friend, then got out her phone. "Brent, I'm taking you up on the offer of a few days off. Brad will be in the hospital today, but home tomorrow and he's going to need help. The last thing he wants is his sister coming over. You don't know her? Well, let's just say she sets his teeth on edge. Yeah, only thing on my schedule is the court Thursday: I'll come in to give testimony and be out until Monday. I can drop by and fill out the paperwork. Thanks, Brent. I'll keep you posted."

She clicked off that call and made another. "Mrs. Malcom? Listen, Brad is in the hospital, no, he hasn't been shot, he got hit on the head and they're keeping him for observation. Yes, he's going to be fine, they're running some tests but the doctor doesn't see any real cause for concern. No, I don't think it warrants his sister Allison coming out. He won't need help cleaning out the house. No, he won't need someone to cook. Lasagne? No, I don't think so, he'll be having clear liquids until the nausea is over from the concussion. It's all under control. They're going to give him something to sleep for tonight; no, Mrs. Malcom, they aren't putting him into a medically induced coma. No, He is not in danger. No, maybe I better tell Allison. Yes, the wedding is still on. No, I am not going to wear a designer gown. I have to get back to work. Goodbye, Mrs. Malcolm. You have a great day and yes, I will keep you posted."

She took a deep breath, a slug of coffee and made the next call. "Allison? Listen, it's Casey. Brad is in the hospital overnight; got hit in the head but nothing serious, it's just observation; he'll be home tomorrow. Yes, I let your mom know first. I've already walked the dog and everything's under control. No need for you to drive all that way. Yes, I know you're a nurse, but he doesn't need another one here in the hospital, they're pretty much fully staffed far as I can see. I'll tell him you know, and he can call as soon as they get back to him with all the tests, oh, you know. You get hurt during work hours and the state makes them do everything that's known to science. Just sort of CYA stuff. He's fine. He shouldn't have visitors tonight, they gave him something so he could sleep, so he'd not be able to talk much anyway and they're sending him home tomorrow. Yes, he has Dr. Michaels, he's a good ER doctor and I don't know who the in-house doc is upstairs is in step-down – no, he didn't have a stroke; it's normal practice to go into step down after a head injury. Yes, his pupils are responsive and no, they'd didn't beat him up or anything, he looks fine. No, his house doesn't need to be cleaned, far as I know, and besides, you and Ruckus don't really get along. No, Ruckus doesn't do well in kennels. Yeah, I can't think of a kennel that would take him for a few days. He sort of goes through their enclosures like a backhoe and honestly, Brad likes him to be home. I don't think he'll be up to lasagna anytime soon. He'll be on clear liquids until the nausea part is done. Yes, nausea from a blow to the head. Yes, so far, it's just a concussion. I can have him call when he wakes up if you want. If he doesn't call, I'll keep you posted. You take care and don't worry, I'll call if anything happens; bye now Yeah, sure you go ahead and call your Aunt. I don't think I have her number anyway. And yes, your mom mentioned the designer gown but really, we have the gown under control. Yes, I'll think about lilies and roses. Gotta go."

She shook her head after the grilling, rubbed her temples and dialed one more time. "Mom! Listen, Brad got hurt, I'm going to be late home, he's OK. He got thumped on the head. No Mom, he's fine. Yes, Mom, he'd appreciate some homemade soup after he gets out of the hospital. No, Mom, we don't need to go clean his apartment to get it ready for him to come home. Yes, I know that makes you feel good, but he's a guy. He'll feel like he's being invaded. The sheriff already took care of the dog. It has to be walked; I'll do that after I finish eating. You remember last time you tried to walk Ruckus? That did not end well. You're lucky he only sprained your ankle and didn't break anything. You just aren't big enough to stop him when he's protecting you from squirrels. Brad's going to be fine, nothing to get worried about, just letting you know I'll be late tonight. Yes, the wedding is still on, he's got a concussion not insanity. I'm sorry I raised my voice. It's been a long day what with the kidnapping and all. Hug Annie for me. You making lasagna? What is it with lasagna? Oh, you're right, lasagna night at Ricci's. Hug my peep for me, can't wait to get home. Bye, Mom."

Sighing, she hung up her phone. She sipped her coffee, took two Tylenol, squared her shoulders and left the cafeteria, drove back to the office to make some calls, fill out leave paperwork, and go back to the hospital. Brad was in Stepdown Unit 3 and the sheriff was with him when she got back.

"Hey, Casey," Erick said. "You OK, dearling?" He gave her a hug.

"Yep. Brad, called your mom, called off the sister, called my mom and took a few days off. You're going to need someone home with you."

"Honey, you didn't have to do that. I'd be fine. I'll bet my crawling skills still exist and I can't fall down crawling."

"I wouldn't be so sure. You won't be able to take Rutherford on walks or anything."

"So the dog needs you?" he smiled.

"And he doesn't make soup."

"If I ever eat again," he yawned. "Not even ice chips are doing it for me right now. The headache's gone but I sure am sleepy."

"Then you sleep. Erick, you got everything you need?"

"Yeah, got his statement, he's signed it, he's got leave coming so I'll fill those papers out. Doc says no office for a week. I'll see you next Friday. Not before, you got me, young man? That turd nearly cracked your brain bucket. I have no time to train a new deputy."

"Next Friday," Brad repeated. "Hey, Casey, you want to get married? I got several days free."

"No! Right now, I have a home visit to walk a monster dog, then I will be back in the morning to take you home. Nurse says you have to sleep. I'll see you for breakfast." She leaned over and kissed him. "And don't think you can get out of marrying me by dying, mister. I got help on the other side."

"It's the Irish in you . . . must be part fae," he muttered back. "I am going to go to sleep right now."

"He's medication naive," said the nurse coming in to check on him. "He's not used to drugs and his body really reacts to them. I doubt he'll move all night. Now, while he's recovering at home, I suspect he's going to be a real pill. Men usually are – and what's this about a dog?"

"That's Rutherford. He has a big dog that needs walked. Here's my card and I've written my home cell on it; please call me if there is any change."

"I'll do that. And the hospital social worker said she'd look in as well."

"Yes, Andy's great. His mom may stop in later, not sure. I tried to stop her but she's sort of a force of nature in his family. Blows up like a hurricane once she gets going."

"Thanks for the warning, we'll watch for her, but he really needs to just sleep."

"I agree. And if you can get her to agree, you're a better man than I am, gunga din, if you get my drift. I'll be home if you need me."

Casey drove by the apartment and found the leash hanging in its usual place. Ruckus was a little uneasy about her taking him out but settled quickly and she jogged over to the park. The children had left for the day, but he was used to dashing up the dog run; she let him go in the dog area and watched. When Ruckus ran, he stretched out and it appeared as if he was half greyhound, half whitetail deer, covering more ground than she thought possible, in long leaping strides, each circle around faster than the last. He ran in a huge circle, around the edges of the fenced-in dog yard, never stopping, faster and faster, then cut straight across the middle and finally pulled up to a stop in front of her, panting and grinning.

"Great day, Ruckus that was astonishing. Here, let's get a drink of water. You need to run again? Or are you ready for the potty run?"

They took off together; she disposed of Ruckus' droppings, put the leash back on, and decided to walk through the park. Ruckus pulled on his leash and tugged her to the left.

"Whoa up there, boy, never known you to get rambunctious on the leash, what is it?" He gave one of his deep-throated woofs, followed by a growl and stopped. She looked around and gasped, fumbled for her phone, speed-dialed a number.

"Sheriff Black speaking." came the rough voice.

"Erick, come over to the park, now. You need to see to this," she reported crisply. "It's not good."

"Do I need an ambulance?"

"It's too late for that, I think."

In less time than she thought possible, the Sheriff was coming up on her location.

"What's the matter Case? Hi, Rufus. What in the name of Pete? That looks like old Mrs. Harmony's dog. And isn't that her cat up the tree?"

The little grey poodle had been killed. A hangman's noose held it in the tree within sight of the school. Tucked into its collar like a cape was another quilt block. The cat, up in the tree, yowled at them, made its way down lower and yowled again.

"Let me call Suzanne to check on Mrs. Harmony. I'll have her bring her here to make a positive ID." Erick talked into his radio a second. "Deputy on duty be here in a sec, I'll go get Mrs. Harmony."

"Do we have to bring her to see this? Poor old thing, this is going to be such a shock."

" 'Fraid so. I've got a towel in the car to wrap the dog in, though. No need it has to be hanging here like that when she comes."

He walked back to the police car, talking on the phone. He came back and after taking a few pictures, cut down the dog, wrapped it gently in the towel, and laid it on the bench in as natural a pose as he could get. He put the noose in an evidence bag. In what seemed a very short time, Suzanne, Mrs. Harmony and half the members of the Yarn Sisters came up the path.

"Mrs. Harmony, I would have come to get you. Didn't have to walk all the way here. Afternoon ladies. Mrs. Harmony, I need to ask you a couple of questions," began the Sheriff, after nodding at the ladies.

"When did you last see your dog?"

"Why is Mia up that tree? Come down here, you naughty girl!" the old lady exclaimed. "To answer your question, I saw them at breakfast. I fed them their breakfast, but this is Wednesday, so I went to the cafe to eat. Wednesdays are Senior special day and I do so love their omelets. Let's see, after that, I went shopping for groceries and such, and then I came back and went to the knitting group at the store. That's where you found me. So I guess not since 7:30. But you surely didn't haul us out of the group just cause somehow my cat got loose?"

"Not exactly, ma'am. Please come over to this bench." He took her arm gently and led her over, the other ladies following. He quietly unwrapped the dog.

"Oh, my Lord!" she cried. "What happened to my Pierre? He was fine this morning. Did he get hit by a car? But how could he get out? My door is locked, the windows are closed."

"I don't think so. We found him this way. We think someone killed him deliberately."

"Who did this?" demanded one of the Yarn Sisters.

"How dare they kill that little dog! He came to meetings and he never hurt a soul," demanded another.

"Erick, you have to find the murderer," said his wife firmly, crossing her arms. "We aren't safe in our own homes. Next time, it could be someone's child."

"Hush, now ladies. I honestly don't know how the perpetrator got into your house, yet, Mrs. Harmony. I have a team waiting to go check that out and dust for prints and look for evidence," replied the Sheriff. "I am going to find out. I just needed a positive ID from you. I'm going to take him to the vet to determine cause of death and then do you want him back to bury him?"

The old lady was holding her cat and sobbing. The cat was snuggled up under her chin, purring almost frantically. The circle of her friends surrounded her.

"Officer, if you bring him back to us after the vet visit, we can see that he's properly buried. I have a place in our back yard we can properly inter the little guy," said one of the sisters. "My old dog Rollo is interred there, and Pierre can be put next to him. They can be friends again in the hereafter."

The ladies moved off. Suzanne, who had come with the ladies, and her sister Alyssa, waited until they were out of hearing. "Is it?"

"Fraid so. This is the patch."

She took a picture. "Crossed Roads. What can this mean? They're kidnapping folks and killing animals?"

"The FBI comes this afternoon. This is beginning to look like hate crimes against the whole town."

Chapter 23

Alex Drummel was driving home from the bank late. He mused over the last few weeks events as he drove, slightly slower than usual; his Prius quiet, efficient, humming along. Word of the killing of Mrs. Harmony's dog had spread and the old lady had been inundated with casseroles and well-wishers. One of the townspeople raised poodles and promised her the best male out of her next litter in the spring. The Yarn Sisters had vowed vengeance on the murderer, and they all knitted small squares that they sewed together for a shroud for the little darling, and Jacob Miller brought her a wooden handmade doggy coffin, nicely made and lined simply with calico fabric. Mrs. Harmony had made his last child a baby blanket and gifted his wife at the store, and Lydia had asked him to make a little coffin box; they saw no harm in kindness to an old lady. The Amish were such good-hearted folks; even if you couldn't agree with their views on modern life, they always helped their neighbors. Mrs. Harmony was so grateful for everyone's care of her and her poor cat. "I live in a good town," he thought. "We all pull together around each other. Even if you're a little bit of a misfit like Ms. Bibby, folks help. I do believe the seniors in town all rallied and brought her food and took up a collection as well. Nice place we live in. Think I'll take the old Folsum road short cut." He turned off, went downhill around a curve and hit a straight place in the road where he sped up a little. A green pick-up truck was coming the opposite way and he hardly noticed it as it passed, then a red car, then for all the world, yes, it was a pumpkin-colored Volkswagen bug. Gave one a start to see so much traffic on this little road. He went up a hill, slowly because there were no Amish buggy roads here, and he'd not want to hit one over the rise. As he came down the other side, he saw a blue car suddenly swing into his lane. Alex honked, swerved to avoid hitting the car but it matched his swerve for all the world like a game of chicken; it came right at him as if the person driving the other car wanted a head-on, he swerved to match and at the last second, Alex swerved one more time but lost control; his car ran off the side of the road, rolled twice and landed on its side.

The airbags went off on all sides and quickly went down. Alex was barely conscious; he heard someone fooling with the driver side door, and then nothing.

When he came to, the car was upright, the door open and he was being taken out by paramedics. Sheriff Black was there with a stern look on his face, the one he got when he thought someone had been up to nothing good. "Alex, you OK? You see who did this?"

"A blue minivan, small, but the guy tried to head on me, and he was wearing a black ski mask. I hit the ditch to avoid being hit head-on and I don't know anything other than that." The paramedics were strapping him onto a stretcher, taking his vitals, hooking up an IV. "I heard someone come over and fiddle with the door, but no one said anything. I don't remember anything else since that."

"Need to get him to the hospital, Sheriff. I'm sorry," said a paramedic. "If you come over, you can probably question him between tests."

The sheriff nodded. He was putting something into an evidence bag. The wrecker came to pick up the car.

"I just got that Prius," groaned Alex. "I had to wait six months for it. The wife is going to kill me. She's wanted one for so long and on the way home from the dealer, here I go, wrecking it."

"I suspect she'll be more worried about you than the car," answered Erick as the medics cranked up the stretcher and rolled it to the ambulance.

"See you at the hospital," Alex called as they locked in the stretcher.

"I'll just see that traffic goes around the wrecker guys and be right along." The ambulance pulled out. Erick looked at the quilt square he'd taken off the dash. "The only MO is the blocks," he muttered to himself. "What on earth is it with the blocks? I'll ask the ladies what this one is but hope the FBI guy can make head or tails of it."

Chapter 24

Brad had been home for three days. He was no longer dizzy. He ate like a horse. Casey took care of him and my! She could cook! It was driving his mom and sister crazy since they wanted to take over the cooking, but Casey seemed always there.

Cabin fever was hitting him bad. He wished he could get back on the job. He'd heard about the dog in the park and was glad 'his' kids weren't there to see it. Mostly, he worried, and fussed, and bit his tongue a lot to avoid snapping at his ever-attentive fiancée; her mother, his mother, his sister, his aunt, her daughter . . . all of whom just wanted to help. He was drowning in a sea of estrogen as the ladies all bickered as they tried to anticipate his needs. He was getting really sick of his invalid status. In a lull in the ladies' voices, he quietly called out. "Casey, you out there?"

"What do you need, honey?" She walked into his room.

"I'm fine. Wanted to take Ruckus for a walk." Brad was sitting up in his room; he'd already dressed, brushed back his hair, and run a shaver over his face quietly while the ladies squabbled in the kitchenette.

"I just got back from taking him to the park. I told the kids you were getting better and might even be back next week. You sure you feel strong enough for a walk?"

"I am feeling fine; no more symptoms and bored to tears." His look was furtive as he glanced past her to the door. "They all still here?"

"Mom, mine, has left to attend a yarn group class. Your mom went to buy chicken to make chicken soup; your sister is out front talking to the newest deputy and assuring him you won't be back for ages and you weren't up to receiving visitors."

Brad groaned, got a determined look on his face and stood up. "That is absolutely it. I am heading out now."

"You want to go to the library? Mrs. Olsen has some new books in, and I hear they're real page-turners."

"If it gets me out of the house, that would be grand."

They both put on coats, put Ruckus on his leash and went out the back way to avoid his sister.

It was late winter, and it looked tired out, the snow not white and pristine anymore, sort of grey or brown in spots, the cars splashed with white salt, everything weary and sad looking. Even the sun was overcast as they stepped outside, came around the front of the building, confusing the new deputy as he saw Ruckus amble past, tail up, head up, a doggy grin on his monster face. The top of his head hit just at the short officer's chest and his tail flicked him on the arm as they turned toward Main Street from Brad's place. The shopkeepers were doing their best to keep the street colorful and inviting, some of the window displays going just a little over the top in this late February weather.

Brad and Casey walked slowly. Brad felt slightly disoriented, not dizzy exactly but his depth perception made him glad he was holding onto a pretty girl's arm. *"Of course, I wouldn't have to feel this way and I'd still be glad to hold onto Casey,"* he smiled to himself.

They walked as far as the police station. Sheriff Black was just getting out of the cruiser. "Good to see you up. You feeling better?"

"Not 100% yet, but lots better," Brad replied. "Thought we'd get a little fresh air."

"You want to step in and get warm, sit down a minute? I need you to meet someone. I was going to bring him around to your place, but you have a crew of Amazons protecting it and I wasn't sure it was an entirely safe idea. However, he should meet the dog before he visits." Brad gave him a quizzical look as he and Casey went inside. "This is Agent Troy Bellows and he's been studying our quilt blocks and trying to figure out what in the world is going on. Here's the square from this morning, Troy."

"Good to meet you, Brad, looking forward to working with you." He scanned the quilt block into a file, put it into an evidence bag, and then into a file with the others. "This is called Bow Tie," he mused as he studied his file online. "Just like all the others, it was popular in the late fifties, early sixties. Whoever is using this is acquainted with or used to make, historical quilts. We've had none of the modern patterns, everything is pre-1995. Most mid 60's, some fifties. I'd say our quilter is probably, OK, this is weird, in her mid-seventies but for a lady that old, or a man, she's pretty darn spry. It has to be a group, maybe a grandma and kids? And the things they do are getting worse. The banker could have been killed in that crash this morning."

Troy turned around in his chair to face them and looked straight in the face of Ruckus who had lowered his head, stalked over next to him, began sniffing Troy's back and peered at him under his heavy eyebrows. Troy gasped, started and leaned back. Ruckus leaned into him and took another whiff. The dog rumbled in his throat and looked up at Brad who nodded. Ruckus sniffed once more and came over to sit by Casey. The Sheriff seemed not to notice.

"Bowtie? The bank president always wears bow ties and so did his dad. Sometimes they're pretty wild colors but his dad's were always a sedate blue or green." Sheriff Black studied the square. "So, this person must have known the old man, using this blue/green tartan plaid for the tie part. This is simply creepy."

"What? They?" interrupted Brad. "Another incident? And they as in more than one?"

Casey interrupted. "Troy, this is Ruckus. He's a trained tracker, best in the country far as I can see, and he takes a little getting used to but he really is a softy at heart." Troy's eyebrows had not come down yet. He turned back to the sheriff.

"He is obscenely big!" he exclaimed. "Aren't most trackers closer to the ground, you know, basset hounds and all that?"

"Maybe elsewhere, but Ruckus is one of a kind. Erick, you were saying?" asked Brad.

"Yeah, another. I've got them grafted now onto a grid; that last Amish cabin one completes the quilt around the top and two sides of the quilt but there is a space for another incident on one of the Amish farms, right here. This farm at the bottom, owned by one of the Hershberger's. You know them?" asked Erick, more for Troy's information than anything else. It also gave him time to study the map with his back to Troy who did not need to see his grin over the dog and Troy's meeting.

"David runs the local grocery and that's his parent's farm, good folks, law-abiding, Old Order Amish. David opened the grocery store when the old one closed down so his people wouldn't have to hire drivers to get to a general store and he's grown it into a pretty nice market. Employs mostly young Amish folks, carries all the regular groceries plus things like lantern mantles and leather strips to repair harnesses, old-time hand stuff like hand mixers and stuff. He's well-liked in the neighborhood. You think his farm is going to be hit next?"

"Well, the pattern seems to be back and forth Amish, then regular folks, and right now the town has been surrounded by attacks, and the edge is almost done. It appears someone's making a quilt," Troy explained.

"That's what Thom and Suzanne think as well." Troy looked at Brad, his eyebrows raised. "Local quilt experts, own the first store that was attacked, here, and they've been useful identifying the quilt patterns for us."

"It's not good to bring civilians into an investigation. Chain of evidence will get messed up," the agent frowned.

"But asking an expert without revealing info is accepted practice," said the sheriff. "And now that you've got that program to identify the patterns for us, they'll not be needed, so all's good. Anyway, you think David or his family are the next targets?"

"I think it likely our protagonists will want to fill in the edge," replied Troy. "The farm would fill it to the edge, but so would an attack on this store – that way the end of the street is filled. He's hitting in clusters."

"He?"

"I know it seems odd to think of a man sewing blocks like this, but men are known to be artistic."

"I guess," replied Brad. He stood up slowly. "I have enjoyed this discussion but I think my bed's calling me. I'll be glad when we're back to normal. I'll be glad when I'm back to normal. I'll be glad when all the women leave my apartment and I did not mean that like it sounded. Casey you aren't a woman, I mean, yes you are, but I mean the two mom's and the sister and the ladies who are dropping off all the casseroles..." Casey smiled and hit him in the arm as he got up.

Erick nodded. "Take care of yourself. If you need to stay home past Monday, let me know."

"I most thoroughly hope not. Love my girl, love my dog, am debating about the other women in my life but I am getting cabin fever. I see the doc Friday and hope I will be cleared to drive."

Brad put his hat on, Casey took his arm and they strolled out of the station.

"He is actually a really good man. His dad was a cop, his grandpa the first sheriff in this little town. He's got law work running in his genes," Erick said as they left.

Troy nodded as he studied the screen. "But that beast? He honestly isn't a tracker? We need to go see the Hershberger's and warn them. I am assuming you have a neighborhood watch here?"

"Yes, we do" replied the sheriff. "So far no real good tips but I've got what's come in stacked here. Mostly after the fact things. Whoever is behind this is good, he sure knows how to be invisible."

"He's really intelligent and he knows his way around the town." Troy considered. "It's got to be someone from the town, who grew up here. It has to be."

The sheriff nodded, "I been thinking that way, myself. If our people are not seeing a stranger, then they're not thinking crime."

"Anyone been away for a while and recently moved back?"

Erick shook his head. "Couple of small-town thugs but we ran them off and I heard they went to Columbus, so no one I know about. I'm heading over to the grocery."

"I think I'll join you. I need to get a better feel for this town."

Chapter 25

"Mom? Mom!" exclaimed the young man as he came to the door with a bouquet. He tried the door and it was unlocked. He came upon his mother in the bedroom, packing a small suitcase.

"Oh, there you are, son," she smiled. "I was packing for my trip to Chicago. I'm just about done. Flowers! How nice!" she chattered as she closed her suitcase. "I want to get to my sister's and back before it's time to put in flower beds. I talked to the neighbor and he's going to bring his rototiller over and till up the ground right there in front by the door and right there in the middle of the front yard. I thought maybe some rose bushes out there and by the house, a few annuals would look nice. And a hanging pot on that low branch out there in front, maybe petunias? And I'll need to buy mulch, so I won't have to weed as much." She had taken the flowers, smiled at her son, and walked into the kitchen, getting a vase, filling it and arranging the flowers to please herself. "Son, are you all right? You usually have something to say."

"You're actually going on a bus to Chicago? Seriously? What if something goes wrong? It's not spring yet."

"Oh, I have that nice cell phone you got me, and I have just about got it figured out. And it's only thirty-nine dollars and it takes eight hours. Sissy is going to meet me at the station with her husband and we're going to go to the Field Museum and the Shedd Aquarium and the Lincoln Park Zoo. And we'll take a day between each thing to rest. It will be so good to see my family. My brother is flying in from New York so it's going to be like a reunion. I will be back in two weeks. Sissy said they'd buy my air ticket back, so I get to mark two things off my bucket list on this trip. Wait, three with the museums." She studied him for a minute. "And I'm sorry, dear, I know you can't get off right now, but I've learned to take pictures with this phone and I'm going to send you pictures of everything. And I'm taking some fabric and my sewing with me and making some squares to remember it all by, and some for you as well. I'd like to complete one quilt before I pass away."

"Mom, don't talk about passing away," he begged. He frowned at the suitcase. "How much stuff is on that bucket list?"

"There is just so much I can do now that I'm not tied to a job anymore. I didn't want to wait, I feel pretty good right now, almost normal, so it's the best time for me to make this trip. I need to get my list done in the next four months so I'm going to be really busy. I want to ride a bus and fly in a plane and go to museums and put in a flower bed by my own home and finish a quilt and enter it in the fair and win one last time and just so many things and there's so little time. Maybe just four or five months until I have to slow way down. I just want to do so much. I want to live before I die." She sat down. "Do you understand?"

Toby took a deep breath and nodded slowly. "I guess I would feel the same way. I just don't like to think of you being gone."

"Did you eat before you came? I don't have much appetite now."

"You've lost weight."

"It's to be expected. I'm ready now to go to the doctor. I'll put my case in the back seat and you can take me to the bus station after. My ticket is for the five o'clock in the afternoon trip. I'll get there in the morning."

"Mom, are you sure?"

"I am certain-sure, dear. Oh, and here are your quilt blocks, I promised them to you before I went. This one is Bear Paw and this one is Sailboat and this one Churn Dash, and Coffin Star and Nine Patch. And I found an Amish pattern as you asked. It's called Amish Pinwheel. I pinned the names to them. I might not have much time in Chicago or I might have time for lots more blocks. Sis has a wonderful Janome machine that won't be tiring to use."

"Does your treadle tire you, Mom?" he seemed concerned.

"Oh, after a while, the treadling gets tiring, but I'm content with it. And I made this little potholder for Dr. Michaels. He's such a nice man and I know doctors aren't allowed to take gifts, but I thought just a potholder, what can it hurt? Let's go now, son. I don't want to be late."

Carrying her suitcase, Toby led her to the car, a curious expression on his face.

Chapter 26

Tuesday afternoon, Brad was at the desk. The sheriff insisted he take desk duty for a couple of days until the all-clear got faxed over from his doctor and Brad was losing his mind. He simply could not understand how his dad, for the last fifteen years of his career, spent so much time at the desk. Right now, he was tabulating the reports from all the incidents, frowning, checking to be sure all the push pins were in the right place, holding the right quilt squares on the map in the correct place and with the dates of incident graphed. The Sheriff and the FBI guy were out investigating a lead.

"Good day, this is the sheriff station," he intoned as he picked up the phone.

"Officer, this is Stuart at the gas station. You have got to get over here pronto."

"What's the problem, Stuart?"

"There's a body hanging from the lift. Francis is having a conniption; it wasn't there before lunch, we came back and there it was, hanging, the lift up. We need an ambulance and you and I've got to go quiet Francis. She's losing it. I saw plenty of bodies in Afghanistan but she's never and she's about, well, she is frantic and weeping and I have to go."

"I am leaving now."

He called Marti and asked her to get an ambulance over to the garage pronto. Then he radioed the sheriff who was on the other end of the township, back talking to the bishop. "Sheriff, you need to wind up whatever happened out there and come in. There's a body in the gas station. I'm contacting emergency services in case the said person is alive."

"What the hell!" exclaimed Sheriff Black. "David Hershberger has gone missing and is assumed to have been kidnapped. I sure as heck hope that's not him."

"I'm almost there and once I see the body, I'll know if it's David. Pulling up to the BP now."

"You're supposed to be on desk duty!"

"Yes, sir, but you're out in the boonies and the murder is here. See you shortly."

Brad pulled up to the pumps and blocked them. He rushed inside.

There, hanging in Francis' garage was an older man's body, suspended from his armpits with a rope. There was a quilt square tucked into his belt. Brad put on his gloves after taking some pictures of the body, the lift, the floor, the garage. "Francis, can you lower the lift just so his feet are touching the ground? I need to check for a pulse."

"I can't go in there," she sobbed. "I can't."

"Not to worry," soothed Brad. "It's this button over here, right?"

"I can get it for you, Officer," said Stuart. "Franny, you wait in the front office. Put up the closed sign. Just drink a soda till I come in." He pushed the button and the lift went down slowly.

"That's close enough," said Brad. He checked for a pulse on the victim's neck. "I'm not getting anything, but I really didn't expect to from the mottled skin and the blueness of his hands," he said. "We'll just put it back up to where it was, good. Let's go in and get your statements. The sheriff and the FBI will be here shortly."

"How did he get here? And so fast! We closed up for lunch, it was such a nice day, we walked over to the park to eat," babbled Stuart, usually a quiet man. "We can see the garage from there, so we could keep an eye on it. Nobody came to the front, and we were enjoying our time and dallied a little, so they must have come in the back." Francis was alternately sniffing and sobbing, her hands shaking around the soda, her face white, taking small sniffs, using up tissues and dropping them in the basket. She was nearly to run out of them, so Francis pulled out another box and sat down next to her, taking her hand. His hands were shaking as well.

"Are you all right, Fran?" asked Brad gently. "I'm just going to let you tell me what happened, I'm going to write it down, and then you sign it. Take your time, we're not in a rush. The ambulance and the sheriff will be here shortly. I hear the siren coming."

"But who would kill Mr. Dickson?" choked Francis.

"Who?"

"He was our old algebra teacher, remember ninth grade? He's retired now. He was always a crabby sort of guy, but he was fair. We all had to suffer through his class, but he never played favorites. He used to come in and get a soda and stand around telling me how to fix cars. I'd just smile and agree then do it my way anyhow. He didn't know what he was talking about but after his wife died, I think he was sort of at loose ends. Why would someone kill him?"

Brad shook his head, "Now that you mention it, that does look like him. We'll have to wait for the proper ID, but it does look like what I remember, a little greyer hair, that's all. Didn't he always wear that same suit when he'd give us tests? That brown one? We used to call it the executioner's suit. I'm sorry. Now, Fran, let's get your statement. Stuart, if you can take this pad and sit over there and write out your own statement? In theory, you're not supposed to be together for the statements, but I don't know about you leaving right now."

"Tell you what," Stuart said. "I'll just sit outside, Fran can see me, and I'll wait for the sheriff while I write. Is that OK, honey?" She nodded. Stuart picked up his pen and the pad and took a chair out to the outside of the window.

"That's a good idea," agreed Brad. "Let's just get your statement, Fran, and you can maybe just rest after that."

She nodded. He carefully took her back over her day, then had her sign the paper. Stuart came back in once he saw they were done and gave Brad his document.

The sheriff came in, lights flashing, as he and the FBI agent jumped out and briskly walked into the garage.

"Yep, sure enough, it's a body," Erick said sourly, hands on his hips, shaking his head as if the idea of a body offended him somehow.

"It's my old algebra teacher, Mr. Dickson, I think," replied Brad. "I took pictures from about every angle and am going to check the back door. The front door was under observation at the time the body must have been put here, so the perp had to come in the back."

"Well, at least it's not Hershberger. His folks are some worried."

"Can't say I feel all that at ease, either," replied Troy. He pulled on gloves, as did the sheriff. They had the lift lowered, checked for life, and went through his pockets.

"His wallet, keys, duct tape, pocketknife, a granola bar, all here," announced Troy. "Duct tape?"

"A lot of folks carry a bit of it around. It's useful stuff. The mercantile carries those small rolls, just the right size for a pocket or purse because you never know when you might need it. We're rural; WD-40 or duct tape fixes everything," explained Erick. He leaned back from patting the back of the victim. "Blood back here but not on the floor, so he was hurt somewhere else and hauled over here to make a statement. Looks like blunt force trauma."

"This guy likes to hit things," replied Troy.

Erick got a call. "Ambulance, coroner, and forensics be here in fifteen minutes. Let's get tape up around here; it's officially a crime scene. I'll check on Brad."

Brad was standing looking at the back door from the outside. "It's the same square as is hanging from the belt, and it's still wet," he announced. He was snapping pictures of the back of the garage. "It's gravel back here so I don't see footprints, I do see drag marks, and it appears a couple of drops of blood here and there. Forensics coming?"

"Almost here. We need tape."

"On it." Brad went to his vehicle, took out a large roll of yellow crime tape and started helping Erick in ringing the area. As he worked, the forensic team came, the ambulance, and the coroner.

The team was efficient: they did their work in less than three hours and the body was taken away.

"Coroner said that death appeared to have been really recent as in within the last couple hours," remarked Troy to Sheriff Black and Deputy Malcolm once they returned to the station. "David disappeared last night and the block there was called Dove in a Window. The one Mr. Dickens is adorned with is called Coffin Star."

"Apropos," commented Brad.

Troy nodded. "You know, you guys don't make bad coffee around here."

"Brad hates bad coffee," answered the sheriff. "I'm going to go over to Mr. Dickens' house and check out what forensics are finding there."

"I'll go with you. Brad, you need to hold down the ship in case, heaven forbid, any more calls come in."

Brad nodded. The other men left. Brad refreshed his coffee and sighed. It was two hours till quitting time and it might have been an eternity. His head was starting to throb again. *"Believe I'll stop by for grub on the way home; that way Casey won't have to cook when she gets there after work,"* he mused. *"We can walk the dog and I'll go to bed and she can go on home and not be bothered. She needs her rest too. Sure am glad to have her help though. And she so nicely got rid of my mom and sister."*

Chapter 27

Thom and Suzanne stood looking at their map, their eyes solemn. Thom added the next patch. "A murder? In this little town?" Thom was perplexed. "I knew it was escalating, but something has to be done. I'm glad we're being kept inside the loop, but the FBI can't be happy about that."

"I doubt Erick's told him. But anyway, who would want a retired schoolteacher dead?" his wife replied. "What is the possible connection between Amish geese, broken windows and murder? What are we missing?"

"It's likely staring us right in the face. I suspect Brad was kidnapped to get him out of the way so the other attack could happen," said Erick coming in. "Elsewise, why isn't he dead too?" He looked at their map. "Yours is pretty much the same as mine. Patches on addresses. Yours has more fabric though. Think I need to cover the streets?"

"We're looking for patterns and it helps Lydia to visualize. She thinks the outside of the crime quilt is full now, except for one person, here. This little farm where old lady Clamons lives. She's not Amish, but she's been a good friend. Her son takes her to appointments and sees she's taken care of, but he's pretty busy. He does live at home. The Amish like that he cares for his mother in her home. He seems a straight shooter."

"What's he do?"

"Well, actually, her son works with Dr. Michaels over at the hospital. I think he's a physician's assistant or some such thing. Mrs. Clamons worked for years at the paint factory. I haven't seen her in ages. She doesn't get out much."

"Didn't she used to sew?" asked Erick. "Years ago, before her husband took off with that floozy from Columbus, I remember she had a bunch of little boys at the time? My mom judged quilts at the fair and said she was the best she'd ever seen."

"I don't know. I think that was before we moved here. I can ask Mrs. Olsen or Mayellen at the post office. They've been here forever. But last I heard her health was going downhill fast and I doubt she can harm anyone."

Erick mused a bit. "I guess not. Odd that she hasn't been hit yet."

"Maybe the criminal has a heart?" remarked Lydia. "I took Mrs. Clamons some cookies yesterday. She's going on a trip to see her sister in

Chicago and is all excited about it. She such a sweet old lady. And I finished shutting the store down and we're getting ready to leave, Suzanne."

"Call it a day then," replied her boss. "I just have to enter the stuff into the computer inventory and get the deposit ready. You two be careful going home."

"My husband is coming to take us home," Lydia said seriously. "We're all being careful. I do wish we could find whoever is behind this." She came over to the map and was joined by Miriam.

"Have you noticed we have the edges of this quilt filled, and that if you look at it and compare the blocks with each other, the more complicated blocks are at the top, here, and the intermediate ones are in the middle and the simple ones to the bottom? I'd almost expect a nine square to be next. I wonder what that means?"

"Good observation. And if you look at events, the events were simpler on this side and are getting, well, more violent on this side. This side had the murder, the kidnapping, the assault, the bank attack; this side had broken windows, blown tires and the cafe fire, the dog killing."

"So, what you're saying is there are patterns but not really easily noticeable ones," answered Erick, who had been taking notes. "if you come up with anything else, let me know."

"I think, if you look at it, something is going to happen here, by the grocery, and here near the church. The church lot and cemetery fill in the outside edge of the town before farmland takes over and you have to look that they tried to run the bank manager off the road outside of town but still within the confines here of the binding. Nothing has happened outside the binding roads, so I think the library, the grocery and the cemetery are going to get something next and if they think of this store as being separate from the guys' stores, Mike and Allyssa are due, too. I could be wrong," Lydia said.

"I see why you think that." The sheriff looked at where she pointed. "I think we've gone past material damages and this person is going to be out for more escalation. Has David Hershberger been heard from? Wouldn't he count as the grocery? He's the owner."

Miriam shook her head. "No, he hasn't been heard from nor has anyone been contacted. He's been gone on buying trips before but always contacts home every evening. And I think his kidnapping happened at the farm. I think the grocery is still going to be hit. I could be wrong. I hope I'm wrong."

"I think the FBI is considering him kidnapped," said the sheriff as he pulled out a small patch and added it to the map. "So, I think the grocery has been hit. Troy says it's called Dove in a Window."

"Then we need to get cracking before anything else happens," said
Thom. "I'll finish locking up and join you by the store." As he turned, Alan
fell into the room. "Mom!" he cried.

"Alan," screamed his mother. She ran over to her son. "What on
earth?" She knelt and took his head in her lap. His arm was bleeding, and his
dad quickly put a pressure bandage on it by folding up a couple felt squares
and holding it tight.

"Look for a guy with a black eye," Alan groaned. "I was going out
the back way to get coffee and he was waiting on the fire escape and tried to
hit me, but I saw him out of the corner of my lenses, and I deflected his
blow. I hit him back good square and he cut me and when I hit the floor he
ran and he dropped this," he handed his mother a patchwork square. "I rolled
down a few stairs and came in the back here. I think it's called a Nine Patch.
Didn't you make one once?"

"Where did he run?" demanded the sheriff. He headed towards the
back, looked around and returned.

Miriam looked at Lydia. Miriam took the patch to the copier and
scanned and printed it, thumbprint then full size, and handed it to the Sheriff.

"Guy ran out the steps in back, but it took me a couple of minutes to
get here. Man, my head hurts." The sheriff ran back out, over to the stairs
and radioed the station.

"I have a footprint, need an ambulance and forensics ASAP," he
shouted into his phone. "Where's Troy?"

Lydia pinned the thumb printed square onto the grid. "Nine Patch,
just as we suspected," she murmured. "And Alan is Mike's son, so that
leaves the library, the cemetery, and Mrs. Clamons as our most likely
targets."

Chapter 28

Troy accompanied Brad on his town walkabout Friday.

"I need to get a better feel for this place. Tell me about the industry in your town," he started.

Brad laughed. "I'd not call it anything like that. Let's see, besides farming, tourism probably supports more people than anything else. The hospital twenty miles from here is the biggest actual employer. There's Craig's Trucking, over on the west side, he has around 11 drivers working for him, they do deliveries mostly for the big chains. Yoder's Furniture makes Amish wooden furniture that ships all over; they have I think all Amish working there, twenty or so. To the south of us, five miles out is the turkey farm. Did you know the Goodyear blimp isn't supposed to fly over turkey farms? Birds are so dumb they think the shadow is a hawk and they'll go about nuts trying to escape it and kill half the flock panicking. Least, that's what I've been told. Let's see now," he paused, waved in the window at Finian, and started to walk again. "We have Carmichael's Paints. They've been here for a long time. Had a lot of OSHA violations before the kids took over from the old man and built a new factory, up to date, all new and mechanized. When they moved, they were able to cut their workforce by 30% due to the updates and a lot of people lost their jobs which made for some hard feelings. Then there's the fiber mill, oh, two miles out, Blue Dawn fibers. They turn sheep wool and alpaca and about anything else you want to grow into roving and yarns. They have twenty-five or so folks working there and are always backed up. Heard Suzanne say they have a six-month backlog of orders to do. Fiber Avalanche carries its yarns. There's all the shops and restaurants in town, of course, and the school are all employers. Our population around about us in the township limits and so on is around 7500, so I think we do well for a small place."

Troy nodded. "This paint factory," he started. "Mrs. Clamons would have worked at the old building, the one with violations?"

"Yeah, I'm sort of a history buff. The old man who started the business, Carmichael, was a tight-fisted fellow. Only fixed things when he had to, didn't pay very well. His boys run a better shop. Anyway, Mrs. Clamons' husband left her high and dry for a woman he'd met working as a salesman for the paint factory. He took the older boys and left. Toby was just a little kid when they lost their house. I remember my dad being all unhappy that he had to hold a sheriff's sale on her place. But Mr. Clamons had run up bills she didn't even know he had and when he left, the bills somehow all came to her, and she went under, declared bankruptcy and the house was sold. It didn't cover everything. She had several jobs trying to make ends meet and pay it all off. They lived in an old trailer for a while, and then Hershberger's rented her the little apartment over the store and she got a job at the paint factory. She worked there for years, raised her boy Toby and he went to the military after high school. I don't know if her other sons ever saw her all those years. I know her ex came back a couple of times trying to get money out of her. My dad ran him off for her when he tried to break in once. He actually tried to get child support once for the older boys. It was one hot mess. What was that kid's name?" He stopped, a thoughtful look on his face. "It's escaped me. I ought to go look up the kid's names but unless they're suspects, it seems a little far-fetched. They weren't even raised here."

"But she survived all that and raised her son and now he's a physician's assistant?"

"Yes, he is. He came back, bought their little house and they moved in. I hear she's dying. I haven't been to see them recently. I see Toby around the stores sometimes. He's civil, hardworking."

"Well, I've pulled his service record. Did you know he was a war hero? Saved his entire unit back in Afghanistan. Got a medal, commendation, the whole bit. I'd like to know the other brother's names to find out where they are. I know it sounds unusual but still, turning over every stone here."

"Can't recall it right over, Larry, Luke, Landon something with an L. We could just ask Mrs. Clamons." Brad nodded to some folks who were shopping as he passed them.

"I suspect we ought to do that." They walked quietly a few minutes.

"Something I've been wondering. You all are about the friendliest little town I've ever seen. Do you have any malcontents? I looked up the last ten years of criminal activity and except for a few shoplifting counts and car accidents, no real crime until this last year. And it does not coincide with Clamons' moving home. He's been here about two years. He lived in Millersburg right after he completed college, did his residency, then just moved in with his mom after buying that house. I looked up the online store she talked about. It does have her quilt blocks on it and only her quilt blocks along with a nice blurb about her winning the fair so much. The ones on the site are exact matches for what's being left at the crime scenes."

"What?" Brad stopped flat in his tracks. "Are you thinking that old dying lady is the criminal mind behind all of this?"

"I don't know. She doesn't seem to know much about computers, the store is run by her son. He works pretty long hours to have time for this stuff.

I wouldn't say it's an alibi exactly, but I don't know. They have the matching blocks. But then, your quilt shop friend Suzanne has the book with the page in it that has all the patterns used so far as well. She has the expertise to make the blocks. She has access to fabric matching the fabric at the crime scenes, and so do her sister, their two helpers and for that matter so do the husbands and son."

"Lydia, Miriam, and Suzanne? Are you serious?"

"I'm thinking out loud about my list of suspects. You got any better ones who have access and ability?"

"What could they possibly have as a motive? They live here, they grew up here, they know everybody. And none of those ladies are strong enough to thump me and knock me out. Well, maybe the Amish, but they'd gone home and they don't lurk about."

"So, it brings us back to the one who makes the matching squares."

"They sell her squares. Maybe that's what the perp is doing, buying the blocks and using them to draw attention away from himself."

"It's possible. Seems convoluted but possible. Where do we go now?"

"I generally go up by the garage, then past the firehouse, then the library. Mrs. Olsen has a couple of books for me waiting, I'll pick them up, go back to the station, check messages, you know, the life of the average small-town deputy."

"Yeah, did that myself awhile. Chose to move on bigger. You ever think about that?"

"No, got too much here. All of it good."

"Well, see you back at the station."

"You need to enlarge your suspect list."

"Maybe. I think I might need to figure out the motive first. There has to be a motive. Wait, could it possibly be that Mrs. Clamons was foreclosed on by the bank that was attacked, that same house was bought by the teacher who was murdered, the deputy whose dad held the sale was kidnapped . . . that old lady and her little boy in her worst hour of need, back when they were just butts of gossip and the town didn't help her like it does everyone now? Maybe that's the motive? Just anger at the past, jealousy, grief, you know, all those old-fangled emotions that make good folks do nutty things? See you back at the office." Troy turned and walked back down the street as Brad watched him.

Brad took a deep breath. *I know these people, are they crooks? Am I too close to my people to not see what he sees? Have I been eliminating people because I know them?*

Chapter 29

"I was wrong," Lydia said to her husband.

"I don't think so. You thought the grocery and didn't realize David had not come back so it was the grocery."

"I didn't see them attacking Alan," she replied softly.

"Alan has been attacked?" said her husband as he drove the buggy. "Your boss's son?"

"Yes, just an hour or so ago; we walked out to the road so you would not block the path for the ambulance. Thom shooed us out, saying the ambulance would need to come to the back door. He's right, of course. His son was hit in the head and he was bleeding on his arm."

Jacob shook his head. "I wonder if it is safe for you to go to work?"

"I think inside the building is safe," said his wife. "Ain't so, Miriam?"

"I think so too. I don't think outside is safe. I think we will not be taking our walks up and down the road at lunchtime."

"No, we won't," agreed her sister. She sighed. "I will miss that. Any word from David?"

"Hershberger?" answered her husband. "No, no word. His family are right worried."

"It's a wicked world we live in," said Miriam sadly. "Attacking a good young man, the murder of an old one, attacking Melody, I just don't know. I thought the FBI was supposed to speed things up and find the culprit."

"They are doing what they can. It takes time. Brad says they are going to pull in more people from Columbus to help." replied her husband.

"I suppose. I am glad for our quiet little farm, though. It will be good to be home tonight."

"Well, there is your home coming up, Miriam." Jacob turned the horse up the drive.

"I can walk the driveway home. No need to pull in." remonstrated Miriam.

"I see your husband walking out to meet you, so I will let you off here. I do not want any of our women or children walking out to the mailboxes or being out front more than they need to be. It is getting too dangerous. The bishop and men got together today at Beiler's for a meeting and have set in some agreements to help keep everyone safe for now."

"What sort of agreements?"

"We stay in groups: we use drivers to go into town when we can: we avoid letting the kinner into the front yards and we make sure older kinner are watching them. No one walks to school now; they will be taken by their Da's. I will take you two women into work for now and pick you up. It's for all our safety we do these things. Now I have a hungry spot in my stomach where there ought to be food, so I am leaving you off with your husband and turning this buggy around for home. He can tell you the rest."

Jacob turned their buggy around and he and his wife began to move away.

"I will see you in the morning," Miriam called softly to her sister.

"Ya. Take care. God be with you."

"And with you." The buggy horse trotted down the driveway, briskly taking Jacob and Lydia home.

Chapter 30

"Are you certain you'll be all right, Mom?" Toby asked anxiously. "I could take a few days off and go too."

"Nonsense. I am so looking forward to this. Your mama's a big girl," she smiled. "Now I know you need to get to work, and my bus leaves in just an hour. I'll sit here, sip my coffee, and wait. My bag is packed and checked in so all I have to carry on is my purse and it's not heavy. You get along."

"I don't like to leave you alone. Have you got your medication?"

"Of course I do. All divided up into days and times of days in those nice little medicine holders you got me, a week's worth and the bottles in my suitcase just in case I stay over."

"I still think traveling alone isn't safe," he argued. "A single lady traveling alone is a target for all sorts of creeps."

"Look around you, son," she chided. "What do you see? An Amish couple, a young lady heading back to college, and the stationmaster. Oh, and a security person. There is nothing here dangerous. You get along. I'll be just fine. The bus comes in a little over an hour."

He kissed her on the cheek, hugged her and turned to go. "Call me when you get on the bus, I'm number one on speed dial. And call me when you arrive. And did you pack your charger?"

"Of course. And I will call you from my sister's car. Don't worry. I need a good adventure."

She smiled at him, patted his hand and he turned to leave. She watched him go, sighed, and sat her coffee cup down in a cup holder. Opening her purse, she took out a quilt patch and began to piece it together by hand. She noticed the security guard watching her oddly. He walked across the station to the station master's office. They held a quiet conversation and the stationmaster placed a call.

"Officer, you remember you asked us to report anything odd and showed us those quilt patches? Well, there's a little old lady here and I swear she is sewing that same fabric. She's leaving in an hour on a bus to Chicago. Yes, I'll watch."

In a short time, Troy Bellows, the FBI agent, walked into the station and over to the desk. The old lady was pointed out and he walked over and sat down across from her, taking out a magazine and hiding a recorder behind it.

"That's pretty fabric," he commented. "What are you making?"

"It's a quilt block for my son. He sells them on his web page. This one is called American Beauty; I just love these colors. My son bought me the fabric. He's such a good boy." She hadn't lifted her head but kept her eyes on the fabric.

"Really? What does your son do?"

"Oh, he's a physician's assistant. He works over to the hospital. He takes good care of me."

Troy nodded, looked back at his phone as if checking data. He waited a moment and then said, "Where are you going?"

"I'm headed to Chicago to visit my sister. I've not seen her in ten years, and we are going to have a right good old time of it. Have you got family?"

"Matter of fact, yes, I do, wife and three kids back in Dayton. Let me just show you," he pulled out his wallet and showed her a picture. "That's my Betsy and Billy, Mikie and Honey."

"They are so sweet! If I ever have grandchildren, I hope they look as nice. And Betsy is such a sweet-looking woman. You must be very proud of them."

He put his wallet back. "I am. Our parents are deceased so they've not got a grandparent. Too bad you can't belong to them. Is your son going with you on this trip?" He looked around.

"No, he has to work. And he has his online store to tend on weekends. Are you going to Chicago?"

"No, I'm meeting a friend coming back. Say, I bet my wife would love some of those blocks. Do you know what the address is for your son's website?"

"No, but I just gave him some new ones to sell. The money he got for them is what I've paid for this trip with; he gets twenty-five dollars each for them, can you imagine?" She looked up at Troy and an odd look came over her face. "I feel like I ought to know you. Isn't that odd?" He smiled.

"I look like a lot of people, and I think those blocks are well worth it. Well, I just guess I'll just have to do a search on the computer for online shops with quilt blocks. Does he sell anything else?"

"He says he is starting to carry other things as well, but mostly my blocks for now. Just a minute, let me look here," she rummaged in her purse. "He wrote down what Kevin said. Here it is."

"Kevin?"

"Oh, he's a nice young man that set up the online shop for him, something called a webmaster? Anyway, yes, here it is. I wanted to show it to my sister. She's a lot better than I am at this stuff. See, here it is, he called it MyMomQuilts.com. He said my sister could see the blocks there." He took a picture of the name and she put the paper away, picking up her block. "I'm going to try and get him several made this trip." she began again as she settled. "I usually make them on my old treadle machine. It tires me out so, but I've made many a good quilt on that machine over the years. It got sold when we lost our house back when Toby was a child."

"A treadle machine? I haven't seen one of them in years. I guess the Amish use them, though. Toby is your son?" Troy had the oddest look on his face.

"Yes, he is. He traced down who bought the sewing machine and they still had it and he bought it back. He is so good to me."

"Really? That was nice of him. You lost your house when he was a boy?"

"Yes, it was sold to the math teacher at the high school. All our things were auctioned off and we were left with next to nothing. My husband left me when Toby was just a boy, and I worked so hard, but I couldn't keep up the payments. I went to work at the paint factory. It was the bank took our house and the old sheriff auctioned it off. I hear his son is a deputy now, Brad Malcom. It was Sheriff Malcom that had to set us out on the street. I felt so bad for him."

"I'll bet you did."

He paused. "Was your husband's name John?"

"Well, yes it was, John Clamons but we called him Jack. We had to move away into a little apartment over the grocery, but I paid off all my debts, and raised my son, and put him through school. He's doing just fine. I hadn't made quilts for years; I used to win prizes in the fair for my quilts, back when my husband was alive, and I was a stay at home mom. When they took everything, they auctioned off my quilts as well. They brought good prices, but it all went to pay the debts my ex ran up. Took me six long years to pay all that man left me with; I don't know where he went, but the floozy he ran off with left him, I heard. Serves him right. Now, why am I babbling on this way? You don't need to hear my story."

He smiled at her. "Yes, I can see how you'd feel that way. A lot of folks find me easy to talk to; not sure why but I seem to elicit that response in folks. Guess I should've been a shrink. May I see some of that fabric? It's really quite striking." She handed it over to him, saying,

"Surely, I've got red and greens and cream and some prints, not all of it's in my purse, just the ones I cut out last night to work on during the drive.

I have them in Ziploc bags. See how nice and tightly woven and heavy this fabric is? None of that cheap department store stuff. Toby says he buys it from a fabric shop over to Berlin called Zinck's."

"Yes, it's really quite nice. I don't suppose you have a scrap of it I could have?"

"Whatever for?" she asked in an astonished voice.

"I'd like to show it to my wife. She loves good fabric."

"Well, let me see," she rummaged a bit and came up with three small squares. "I took these along just in case I lost a piece. I have more in my suitcase though. You tell your wife I hope she visits my son's online shop. She can see all the blocks I've made since I retired on the webpage and he put pictures up of our cottage and some of the pictures of me winning prizes I had in an old album. Computers are really the most amazing things. I know I'm early for retirement, but I got ill, and the doctor thought it best, but it's all good. I can do some of the things I've always wanted to do but couldn't."

"You're ill?" his face wrinkled in concern.

"Oh, don't worry, it's not catching. I have cancer. When I get back, I'm to sign up for hospice. My son is fighting that, but I think it's for the best, don't you?"

The agent drew a long, deep breath and he nodded. "Yes, it might be. My name is Troy Bellows. I'm so sorry. I ought to have introduced myself. I have my mother's maiden name instead of my dad's."

"Really? My name is Marie Clamons. Toby bought our old house back from the math teacher about six months ago, and we live just out of town. The math teacher moved into town to be closer to people. I like it out where we are. There are Amish farms on all sides and they are such nice folks."

"Yes, they are. Well, the person I'm meeting ought to be getting off the bus soon. You have a good trip."

"I think that's my bus pulling in. It's been good to pass the time of day with you." She smiled, taking the handles of her chair in her hands, shoved herself up, closed her purse, picked up her sewing bag, took her cane and made her way to the line waiting to get on the bus from Chicago.

Troy checked his pocket and turned off his recorder. His phone rang and he went outside to answer it.

He went to the stationmaster and made some arrangements, then headed back to the sheriff's office.

Chapter 31

Early next morning, Sheriff Black was just getting up to do his rounds when he was startled by the bishop and Enoch Miller coming into his office.

"Sheriff, we need to report a disturbing problem," began the bishop.

"My frau is missing!" blurted Enoch. "She went out to take care of her morning chores and did not come back. I smelled the breakfast burning and went in to find out what was going on and the back door was open and she was gone. I turned off the fire, removed the pan and stepped outside. I've looked everywhere."

"We went by the store and it's locked up tight still," replied the bishop as he laid a restraining hand on Enoch's arm. "I am afraid we have another kidnapping."

"Did anyone find a quilt patch?"

Just then Suzanne and Alyssa came in. Alyssa held out a piece of fabric.

"Sheriff, we found this on the tie out in the back of the store. It's a Bear Paw pattern. I looked over the store, but nothing was out of place, nor at Thom or Suzanne's. Why would he leave a patch where nothing happened?"

Quickly she saw Enoch and her face turned white. "It's Miriam, isn't it? She was supposed to come in this morning with Lydia and neither of them has come."

"I'm here," said Lydia. "No one was home but the kinner and grandparents at Miriam's, so Jacob brought me in."

"Miriam is gone," Enoch's voice quavered. "My frau is missing."

Jacob immediately went over to him, as did Lydia.

"We're not safe on our farms. They took her right out of our kitchen." blurted Enoch.

"But your farm was not on the binding," protested Lydia. "This is out of the pattern."

"Actually, yes, it is," replied Brad. "Look over here at the auditor's map. Your farm, Enoch, is behind the binding farms except for this little strip of woods that come out just at the corner next to the widow Clamons. And Miriam worked here in town at one of the Main Street stores. It fills in another small space. I have to say whoever it is, is surely thorough."

He took a picture of the bear paw quilt block, sent it to the printer, shrank it, dated it and added it to the map.

The phone rang. The sheriff picked it up and spoke quietly.

"Agent Troy has a lead. He's on his way back. He wants us to pull up the grid of dates, places and times and print it out large for him. He'll be here shortly."

"Well, let's see," Brad opened the computer file on the incidents and began to prepare the printout.

Chapter 32

Casey snuggled a little closer as they watched the movie credits. "Annie was bummed out when I told her we were going to the movies and she couldn't come."

"It's a school night."

"And she pointed out it was a work night."

"She has a point."

"But more importantly, we'll be talking about the wedding afterwards."

"I told you I don't care if we get married naked on a beach, and come to think of it, that does have its good points," Brad nuzzled her neck. The lights came up and he sat back.

"We are not going to be on a beach. We're going to use the church in town; Brad, the ceremony is just three weeks away, and I have the florist set up, and the cake ordered, and we sent out the invitations two weeks ago. The RSVP's are coming in," she smiled as they exited the theater.

"Now I want to go over the menu with you, and have your guys all got their tuxes ordered?"

"Tux? I'm wearing one of those cummerbund things?"

"Absolutely. You will be gorgeous. And we already discussed that."

"I know, just kidding. And thank you for not choosing the one with all those frills down the front. We'd look perfect fools in ruffles. A purple cummerbund is strange enough."

"It will match the lavender and pink flowers in the bouquets. And the bridesmaids are in pink and the matron of honor in lavender and the flower girl is in white with a purple sash. You'll all look just wonderful Isn't it exciting?"

"I guess. Can't wait for the honeymoon to get away from it all."

They walked holding hands slowly down the street, pausing to look in store windows as they talked. "We'll be having a rehearsal dinner after the practice on the 18th, and the wedding is the 20th at five," she said.

"I'll put it on my schedule."

"Brad!" she exclaimed. He grinned at her. She went on. "I haven't been able to find a photographer. There just aren't any. We have only two in the entire area, and they're booked. Do you have any ideas?" They arrived at her car.

He paused. "Yeah, but you won't like it."

"Why not? We're pretty desperate right now." They came to a corner and waited for an orange Volkswagen bug to pass. On the other side, near her car, he continued his thought.

"He's an old army buddy. He's a photographer for a news journal, but he freelances."

"Wait," she said slowly. "You mean Alfred? The shaggy-haired guy who always wears tennis shoes, tall, skinny, shaves when the fit hits him, sweatpants and granny glasses Alfred? That Alfred?"

"Yeah, he's won prizes for his pictures, you know. He won a Frelens award for photojournalism just last year."

"Those were war pictures."

"Yeah, but you know, weddings are sort of like battles."

"Brad!" she protested. He opened her door and she got in, fastened her seat belt as he got in to drive. The conversation continued.

"OK, so less blood. I'm pretty sure he'd clean-up for this."

"He attracts flies and he always has a couple of skinny models as assistants."

"Yeah, he tends to attract gold-diggers."

"Mom will have a fit if they show up. I mean, she is really looking forward to this wedding."

"Yeah. But if he's cleaned up, she won't recognize him. And I could be his assistant."

"Brad, you're the groom. You can't be a camera assistant and be at the altar."

"Yeah, there is that. I can ask him to bring Judith Lee instead of the gold diggers."

"The gay guy with the beard and dresses and the red-soled Louboutin shoes?" she gulped.

"He's not gay, he's trans, and he's not a bad person. He does tend to wear capes."

"I didn't say he was bad, but it's a little off-putting to be upstaged at your own wedding by a man in a beard with spiked heels."

"OK, so maybe Alfred won't need the assistants. I'll see if he can work alone."

"He does own something besides sweatpants?" she said anxiously. "I can rent him a tux."

"He won't wear one. When he went to get his journalist award, he wasn't in sweats."

"What was he in?"

"I think it involved a tie and short-sleeve plaid shirt, maybe a sweater?"

"At a formal awards ceremony?"

"Yeah, well, you know, he is from Australia." He pulled up in front of her house and parked in the driveway.

"I thought New Zealand." She replied.

"Somewhere that direction. You know, south."

Casey drew a long breath. "OK. Ask him. We're desperate. I hope he's not too expensive or too eccentric and I'll just tell Mom I have an award-winning photographer from out of town coming in." They sat for a few minutes, each lost in their own thoughts. Finally, he started in again.

"Good thinking. Let me call him when I get home before you tell Mom. I need to take my car back, get the dog and walk him, and when I get home, I'll call. Everything is going to be just fine and this is going to be the prettiest wedding you'll ever be in. Can we neck now?" He turned to her with a smile.

"It's a work night." She smiled at him. "It's a terrible example for Annie."

"Yeah," he said moving closer. "I was thinking maybe go in late to work? And Annie is in bed."

"Brad, I have court at nine tomorrow . . . " She leaned over and kissed him on the chin.

"I have the FBI at 8." He cuddled closer.

"You have a murder investigation tomorrow," she protested as he nibbled at her ear.

"You got to argue with the public defender. I think that's so sexy," Brad murmured. "Anyone who can get the goat of a lawyer regularly gets my vote."

As they were getting a bit more intent on their present situation, the door suddenly came open and a flashlight was shined on them.

"Oh, gross, Mom. I need help with my algebra homework. Do you guys have to do that in public?"

"Young lady, you are supposed to be in bed."

"So's Grandma. She can't do the algebra either. She's watching from the porch."

"You do know we'll be doing this gross stuff after we get married?" asked Brad, sighing as he let go of Casey.

"But it won't be in public."

"We aren't in public now. Turn off that blasted flashlight."

"You-hoo," called a voice. "Are you OK, Casey?"

"Now we've done it. We woke up the neighbor lady. She's a real snoop." grumbled Casey. She turned to Casey and got stern. "Young lady, you go inside right now."

"OK," she said cheerfully and called out, "It's OK, Mrs. Matthews. It was just Mom and her boyfriend making out in the dark."

"Annie!" exclaimed her mom in a stage whisper.

Annie waved cheerfully and sauntered up the walk. Brad glared at her. Casey sighed and said, "Brad, I'll see you at lunch tomorrow, alright? I'll come to the park."

"Sounds reasonable. Not private enough but reasonable." He bent over and gave her a very long kiss. A light came on in the darkness.

"Blast it. Mom's turned on the porch light." The porch lights came on over at Mrs. Matthews and on the other side of the street as well. Casey groaned. "How did I end up having all these concerned neighbors?"

Brad sighed. "We are going to have a honeymoon alone, right? No kids or neighbors or relatives allowed?"

"Long as you don't tell your mom or Allison where we're going. By the way, where are we going?"

"Less said the better. Loose lips sink ships. My ship's not sinking." He smiled. "Pack bikinis."

Chapter 33

"There's stairs, watch your head," growled a voice.

Blindfolded, Miriam was shoved into a dark basement, through an outdoor storm door, and she heard it clank shut above. She fell on the stairs and stopped herself from rolling, then cautiously slid down until she touched the floor, which was cold and slightly damp feeling. Her hands were no longer tied, but they felt numb from being tied so closely. She reached up and pulled the duct tape off her mouth and her eyes, wincing as her eyebrows lost some hair. There was dull light from a hanging lantern.

Against the far wall, a man slowly stood up. "Miriam, wie geit's?" he asked softly. "I don't think they can hear us. Did they hurt you? Where's Enoch?"

"David?" she asked in astonishment. "I'm so glad to see you are still alive! Where are we?"

"In someone's cellar," he replied. "There's a water faucet over there, and I've been eating apples and cabbage for the last couple days – seems this is a working cellar, but not wanting to eat anyone's winter stores and have no way to heat it up, so I've just been eating the raw things. Oh, and finished a head of cabbage this morning, so we aren't starving while we're being held. There is more cabbage and apples, and the faucet. There's a couple cans of kerosene and matches over here on this bench so I have kept the lantern burning low. It gets cold at night. I have one blanket, but they tossed down a bundle with you."

"I didn't see it," she turned and picked it up. She unrolled it. The bundle was a blanket rolled up and tied over a jar of peanut butter, a spoon, a round loaf of artisan Italian bread, a round of lacey swiss cheese, granola bars and a couple bars of chocolate.

"Well, I have a blanket now as well. I think if we are careful, we shall be able to eat for a few days, and we have water, so we'll not starve."
"Everyone has been so worried about you, David Hershberger," Miriam said as she put the food on the bench.

"I can't say I've been happy to be here either," he said. "And I could surely do with some company, but Enoch has got to be worried."

"As I am," she replied. "Let me make us both a sandwich. Do we have any jars we can use as glasses for the water?"

"There were some pint jars empty in back and I washed them out to use. No plates though."

"That's fine. Let me look . . . thought so." she wandered over to the jars and jars of preserved foods. "Here we are," she was almost triumphant. "Whoever put these up, she made jelly. Let's have peanut butter and jelly sandwiches."

"I have to warn you there are mice down here." replied David. "I've found myself talking to them this morning. They'll get into the food we just got."

She paused a moment and considered. "Well, I don't like mice particularly. I'll look around after we eat and see if I can find some way to keep our food safe. By the way, what do you use for, well, facilities?"

"There are two rooms down here, this one, and the one just over there. I found some five-gallon paint buckets with lids. It smells pretty awful but if you keep the lid on it's not too bad. When you use it, it might make you gag." She nodded. She completed a sandwich for herself and two for David and handed them to him. He ate like a famished man who had been surviving on apples and cabbage. She walked around looking for what might be useful, found some empty pickle crocks, and hauled them over. After she'd completed her sandwich, she washed one of the crocks and turned it up to dry, then the other. She walked around again and came back with some old rags, mostly worn kitchen towels which she washed out and hung over the edge of the bench and sink to dry. She tore them into rough eight-inch squares. Finishing this, she took the driest crock, set it upright and put the food in it, covering it with the lid; turning the other up, she did the same thing.

"Well, unless they can move crockery lids, I think I've secured the food stores." she paused. "David, I washed and prepared these little rags to be used for cleaning yourself after using the buckets. I somehow suspect that there isn't any toilet paper here?"

David blushed. "I've sort of been washing my hands after and doing the best I can. So, after I use one of these, bring them over and wash them?" he asked.

"As well as we can without soap."

"Odd you'd say that. I found a crock, let's see, here and it has what looks to be soap in it."

She took a look and smiled. "Whoever owns this basement has grated up soap to use in cleaning, and this is her laundry soap. Let me put a scoop of it right over here for us to use. That will work fine." she hesitated. "David, have you seen our kidnapper?"

He shook his head. "I know he has a handgun and a hunting knife. I have seen them. He opens the door occasionally and tells me to turn my back and I've seen those as he goes around me. He's hauled out the latrine bucket twice. One trip he saw I was shivering, and he tossed down the blanket. Then he tossed you down and the bundle. That's all he's been here. He hit me with something when I was emptying trash out back of the store and I blacked out and woke up in here with the lantern burning. There's no windows or anything. I don't know how many days have passed or how far we went."

"It's been a week since you were gone. Since that time, there's been one murder."

"Murder!" he exclaimed.

She nodded. "One of the English, a retired teacher, was killed. David, it's so dangerous right now."

He stared at the floor thinking.

"And we don't know what's going to happen to us." she continued. "We've seen a sort of pattern, but it hasn't helped us to stop it." she paused. "I wish we had a Bible. It would be a comfort."

"We have what's in our heads," replied David. He went into the other room and came back with two buckets which he turned over near the lantern. "I'll start. My favorite verse is Micah 6:8. 'He has shown thee, oh man, what is good, and what does the Lord require of thee? But to do justly, and to love mercy, and to walk humbly with thy God.'"

"The Lord is my shepherd, I shall not want," Miriam started softly. David nodded and listened, then joined in. "He maketh me to lie down in green pastures: he leadeth me beside the still waters. He restoreth my soul: he leadeth me in the paths of righteousness for his name's sake," she faltered and drew a deep breath. David smiled encouragingly and continued, she joining in, their quiet voices together, getting stronger. "Yea, though I walk through the valley of the shadow of death, I will fear no evil: for thou art with me; thy rod and thy staff they comfort me. Thou preparest a table before me in the presence of mine enemies."

After a pause, David repeated, "Yea, though I walk through the valley of the shadow of death, I will fear no evil: for thou art with me; thy rod and thy staff they comfort me. Thou preparest a table before me in the presence of mine enemies."

They lowered their eyes to the floor and entered a period of silent prayer before David started again. So they spent most of the afternoon, taking comfort in what they knew, putting aside their questions and fears and communing with the One they knew so well.

Chapter 34

The car drew up to the front of the Rose Garden Bed and Breakfast. An older middle-aged man got out of the car, went to the trunk and pulled out a suitcase and garment bag and carried them to the front door. By the time he'd gone through the gate, under the trellis covered in early floribunda roses in yellow and white, the B&B owners, Beth and Franklin were on the porch to greet him.

"Good morning, Mr. Drummel. So glad to have you visit." smiled Beth.

Franklin reached over and took his suitcase. "Visiting the grandkids?"

"I can't believe they're getting so big! Little Alex the Third is 7 and Marcy is four. Careful of the suitcase, I sort of overindulged in some presents. It's my son's wife's birthday, you know. We're going out to dinner and I'll fly back tomorrow."

"Going to visit the bank?"

"No, my son runs it now. Heard he had some excitement recently, but nothing our intrepid sheriff can't take care of. I'm not going to interfere. He's his own man, and I'm so proud of him." Alexander Drummel, Sr. followed them into the house, signed the guest book, and accepted his key. "I do so like this room overlooking Main Street with the little balcony," he smiled. "My wife always enjoyed it when we came down."

"I heard about the accident and I am so sorry for your loss," replied Beth. "She was a sweet lady."

"Yes, to die in a car accident like that was quite a shock. Still, it was a blessing in a way. She'd been diagnosed the week before with stage four cancer and was not looking forward to a good prognosis. At least getting killed on interstate 71 was fast. They tell me she didn't suffer."

"Again, I am so sorry."

"Her last days were busy ones; she was on several boards; she'd talked to me just that morning about working to get a grant for the local library this summer. She had plans to work for charity until she wasn't able anymore. Now I'm trying to fill her shoes a little. I'll be talking to the librarian while I'm here about a bit of a memorial to set up for her. My son

Alex loved that library before he got as busy as I was when I was president of the bank." He smiled. They climbed the stairs and stopped at a door the innkeeper opened for him.

"This room feels almost like home." Mr. Drummel looked around the room. The Sweet Briar suite had double French doors leading out to the little balcony over the porch. The wallpaper was ivory-colored with embossed roses, and there was a fresh bowl of roses sitting on the oak dresser. The floor had a deep plush green carpet. The bedspread on the huge queen sleigh bed was ivory chenille. Off to the right was a bathroom done in creams and light green, accented with red roses, with gold fixtures on the white marble sink. There was a double shower with the walls covered in white sparkling polished marble stones.

"When will you be meeting with your son?" asked Franklin, the innkeeper as he was opening the window shades and doing a quick check to be sure it was all to his liking.

"I'm going to swing by and go to his house at 5; I have a few hours and thought I'd do a walk around the old town. I like to see what's developed since last time. Might see my grandson by surprise in the park at lunch. He always enjoys finding me by accident. I'm going to change into more comfortable walking shoes and might grab a few gifts and definitely stop for a hamburger at the diner. Last time I saw my son was at the funeral and hardly got time to talk. I want to spend some quality time over the next couple of days. If I should want to stay longer, is the room available? A lot depends on their schedule, not mine. I'm just an old retired guy."

"I'm sure that would be fine, but I'll check our schedule." Beth pulled her phone out and scrolled. "You could keep the room until Monday at 11. We have someone coming in for Monday night."

"Then let's just set that now. One night here is not enough." He smiled, "Now if you will excuse me, I've got to get my shoes changed. I've got a burger to hunt down and eat and a grandson to make late to class."

Chapter 35

Troy, Brad, and Erick studied the map. "I'm guessing the next incident will happen either here, to fill out this side of the street, or up here," Erick said. "I hope they aren't murders."

"I want to try something," replied Troy. "Get out the fabric squares and let's go over to your friend's quilt shop. I want to see something."

"Thought we couldn't use civilians?" asked Brad.

"They have a tool in back the shop that ought to help this along."

Grabbing the box of squares, Troy went over to the Fiber Mavens and walked in. Erick stayed on post and Brad went out to watch the areas they were worried about.

Brad muttered to himself as he walked his beat. "The church has been hit twice. So have the fiber folks over there. Of course, the second time could have been to cover the quilt store; the first the fiber store, the hobby store has been hit, sort of fills that block except for the museum. Haven't hit the museum store. No one else has been hit twice, but if you look at it that way, they haven't either and they may be up for one more hit. Lordy, I hope not. If anything happened to Thom or Suzanne or Alyssa or anybody over there, no, no, to make this thing go together, they'd have to hit either the Rose Garden, the Library or I think Finian's. This block has been hit lightly, and the murder victim wasn't a store owner, he just had a house end of Main Street. The house on the other end of Main Street is a rental and nobody's there right now. Checked that last night, nobody in there. So, this block here is up for attack but what is going to happen?"

A pumpkin orange Volkswagen drove past. The young man inside was heading out of town, turned at the stop sign, most likely headed for the state route. A few more cars went by. Brad walked slowly, savoring the spring, looking at the street. He came to the park and checked, kids were all inside and until he checked the park just before they were due to go out, they would be kept inside. No need them to see someone's dead cat if that happened. Darndest thing, killing that little poodle, stringing it up in the park. Sick bastard was what he was, whomever he was.

He looked at the Volkswagen as it went around the block and passed him again, then drove out of sight. In the back of his head, something was bothering him, nagging him. Something that ought to be evident, but he couldn't pull it to the front. He strolled down the street to the Oakhurst Bed and Breakfast.

He walked up the paving stones and knocked at the door. "Morning, Sandra. You got a minute?"

"Surely, Deputy, you come right in. Our last guest just left, and I was going to go clean up the rooms and be ready for tonight's reservations."

"Did one of your guests drive an orange bug?"

"Well, actually, yes. He's a nice young man here on business. He's been coming for the past few months to attend to business. Always polite, doesn't leave a mess. He's booked reservations through to June, every two weeks or so spends a few days and leaves. He's quite the regular."

"Is he related to anyone in town?"

"Not that I know of," she replied. "Coffee?"

"No, got more walking to do this morning. We're cautioning everyone to be careful. If you have security lights, have them on, if you don't have a security system, seriously consider putting one in."

"We have that already installed. Odd you mention it though."

"Why?" asked Brad.

"Our recurring client has a security business. I have his card here somewhere," she looked in her desk, then stuck a business card in her copier and made a copy, giving it to him.

"Here it is. Matthew Solomon, Security Systems Inc. His company is from Hartford, but he works out of Cleveland."

Brad took the copy. "Thank you and keep your eyes open?"

"Will do," she said as she ushered him out the door. He continued his beat past the general store.

Chapter 36

Troy walked into the Fiber Avalanche. Lydia greeted him.

"Any word on Miriam?" she said anxiously.

He shook his head. "No, but I wanted to ask if you could help me a moment?"

"Certainly. What can we do?" replied Suzanne.

"Do you have a quilt layout board?" he asked. "You know, one of those big felt or something boards with a grid on them to put pieces on for planning?"

"Surely do."

"Do you have some fabric in the town colors?"

Suzanne looked at Lydia. "I didn't know we had town colors."

"Let me put it another way. Is there a color that is always used at ceremonies locally?"

"No, pretty much we use what's appropriate."

"Then do you have school colors?"

"Yes, those we have. The school colors are gold and silver." He shook his head. "Let me see the strips you have. FBI will reimburse for this."

"I think the closest we could come would be dark yellow and brown as far as the school colors. Most quilters don't use solid shiny gold or silver. Here's our display of strip colors. Do you see any that might work?"

Studying the strips, he considered then chose several colors. He held them up to show her and she said, "Lydia, show him the design wall grid we use. I'll see to the customer just coming in. Hello, Mrs. Harmony and Mrs. Olsen, so nice to see you again!" Suzanne went to greet her customers, Lydia and Troy went to the classroom.

Lydia quickly took down the blocks that were in the planning stage on the wall. "It's magnetic and pieces are held up with these little magnets," she explained to Troy. He nodded. "We made our wall to our specifications with the guys' help. Most of them are 60 x 72 inches; we made ours a bit larger so that we could use it in classes. It's 72 inches high, 96 inches long."

"Then let's put this in place as a town map." he studied a minute. "If we use each 9-inch square for a business or place, we can grid out the town in blocks and see what happens."

"Haven't we done that with the thumbprint map?" asked Lydia.

"I know, I've been told about your map, but I think life-size is going to make this seem more realistic." He started putting in the roads using 2-inch strips.

"We'll use the solid dark cream for streets, darker ivory for outside binding and put the proper number of buildings along the main street. I cut out paper 9-inch squares last night as spacers." Studying the squares, he first outlined the town with the binding. He put the farm squares in their proper places and put spacer blocks between them wherever no crime had occurred.

"You can go back to work, you don't have to watch me," he said to Lydia.

"It's interesting," she replied. "It sort of fits but the 8 by 12 grid is not working. The normal 9-inch square quilt is 8 x 12. You need to change that to fit what is actually happening. This quilt is not a regular quilt; it's what we call a landscape quilt. People make them to show old childhood towns, commemorate town events, that sort of thing. They aren't really regular."

"How?"

"All quilt squares don't have to have binding between them, like streets. Let me show you. Except for the middle strip, it's working." Quickly she reassembled the squares. "See? This is master level work. The different patterns blend in together and match. And look here? The colors are patterned as well; the darker quilt blocks are centered up here, by this corner. They slowly lighten down to the corner where they're almost pastel. It looks like a cloud is coming over the sun – Sun and Shadow we call that in quilting. And see? This end is finished with the death of the teacher: he was the last patch down here. There are three missing places, Finian's, the Rose Garden Bed and Breakfast, and Mike's Not Your Normal Antique Store. And the excitement we had at the bank is out of sequence."

"Excuse me?"

"Look, it doesn't match the color shading sequence. I am wondering if it needs to be shifted like this," she moved a blank square up, moved the bank square down. "Now the shading is correct. Everything is in order."

"You missed a place." He commented.

"Oh?"

"The widow's place. No one has attacked her. Of course, she's in Chicago right now visiting her sister."

"How do you know that?"

"We have ways," he smiled. He stepped back. "I can't leave these here. I just need to take a few pics." He took pictures from several angles. He leaned back and studied it. "The dates are not a pattern. Some are clustered, some are weeks apart. There is a definite pattern in colors. Is there a pattern in the style of block? I don't see it."

"Yes, there is," replied Suzanne coming in from the front of the store. "All the blocks I see up there were popular as retro in the 1980s. The patterns are older than that but if you look back to the 1980s, these were the most used patterns."

"How would you know that?" he asked.

"Quilt history is a specialty I teach," she smiled. "The college in Ashland has a course in fiber history in America and I wrote the book for the class," she went over to the bookcase and pulled out a book. "After it was published, the college prof saw it, called me, invited me to come to teach the class every year when it's offered, using my book. He said it was the most complete and logical treatise he'd ever seen on the subject," she shook her head quietly, somewhat embarrassed. "I still have the letter and I read it sometimes when I wonder if I'm accomplishing anything at all, like during tax time. It's also good for intimidating rivals and making my kids work harder to match up with their old mom. Here, let's look."

She opened the book about halfway, thumbed a couple of pages. "Yes, here it is. All of those blocks are on this page in the book. I have a page for every era. Whoever is doing this has something to do with the 1980s. The only other ones I can see not used," she looked up and down and lightly drew a pencil line around some blocks. "Churn Dash, Sailboat, Amish Pinwheel, and Compass. He or she has used all the others."

"May I have a copy of this page?"

"Do you one better. I have an autographed copy of my book." He took the page, his box, and her book, and was just starting to leave when his phone rang. He put everything down and answered it; then grabbed it all up again and headed out at a very fast walk.

Erick was sitting in his office when the station phone rang. The voice on the other end of the line was frantically trying not to babble. "Sheriff, you need to come now. There's a body on the altar."

"Excuse me? Who is this?"

"This is Pastor Primo. I came in to work on my sermon, went into the sanctuary and there's a body in the pulpit."

"Be right there. Don't touch anything."

He radioed. "Brad, Troy, go to the church immediately. We have another murder."

Thank you for reading the first book of our mystery series. Here is the first chapter from the next book in the series, Criminal Quilting:

Chapter 1

The ambulance arrived just as the officers pulled in. "Dispatcher is calling in forensics. We need positive ID," ordered the Sheriff.

Troy took pictures: Brad ran around marking off the perimeter with yellow police tape. Erick talked to forensics on the phone giving more directions and took a statement from the Pastor.

"I can't believe it. I just got here and walked up to get my pulpit tablet to start entering my notes for the Sabbath sermon and there he was, draped over the pulpit." The pastor had calmed somewhat from his call earlier. "But my sermon tablet was gone from where I keep it on the pulpit- see, I have this holder that swings out as I need it and instead of my Lenovo I found this Apple. It's not mine and I can't open it. I don't have the passwords."

The sheriff whipped out an evidence bag and slid the tablet into it. "There's a chance it belongs to a parishioner?" he asked.

"It's possible but I found it in the pulpit. Normally no one comes up here. Kids sometimes do, little ones but their mom's shoo them down. The Choir director does practice from over there where that tape on the rug marks her spot. Choir stands back there but they don't practice until this afternoon. Oh, dear! The body will be gone by 3:00 won't it? I can't imagine the choir ladies' reactions to a body. I can ask Sunday and fine out if anyone misplaced their tablet and took mine." The Pastor was beginning to come unglued again. At al look form Erick, Brad led him away from the pulpit and down the three steps to the stage.

"Pastor, let's just go back to your office," he said soothingly. "I have some paperwork I need to have you sign and such, the forensic guys will take care of the problem in here and the church will be ready for the afternoon meetings here. It's only eleven. Is your secretary here?"

"She takes Friday's off. It generally gives me quiet time to polish the sermon." The Pastor wiped his forehead with his handkerchief. "I need to call the wife. If she sees all that yellow tape out there, it could cause problems."

Brad led him to the office, took him inside and shut the door. He gave him a statement pad to write down what happened and had him sign it. He suggested calling the prayer chain for the church and they worked out what he would say to them; then he called the choir director and had her change practice to much later, six o'clock, to be sure everything was back to normal.

"I was going to talk about fear," remarked the pastor. I had my verse all ready, John 14:27 was going to be the Scripture for the day, Peace I leave with you; my peace I give you. I do not give to you as the world gives. Do not let your hearts be troubled and do not be afraid. And I was going to use John 1:9 Have I not commanded you? Be strong and courageous. Do not be afraid; do not be discouraged, for the LORD your God will be with you wherever you go." But I really don't see how I am going to preach with that image of that poor man in my mind." He groaned and put his head in his hands.

"Do pastors have pastors?" asked Brad gently.

"What?" asked the Pastor.

"You know, backup?"

The Pastor wrinkled his forehead. "Yes, that is a very good Idea. I will call my Bishop and explain what happened and get his advice. Perhaps he will have someone else speak for me or may do it himself. Bishop Michaels is a very good man, his brother is a doctor and he has studied counseling extensively. Yes, that is a wonderful idea. I was too rattled to think of it. I will call him right now."

"Will everything you say be confidential? This is a murder investigation."

"Oh, Lord, yes, counsel between pastors is sacrosanct-we have our own version of HIPPA laws, so to speak. Thank you so much."

"If you'll be ok now, talking to the Bishop, I need to go back out."

"Yes, yes, of course. I'll be speaking with my counselor."

By now the forensic folks had arrived and laid the body out on the floor on a tarp. The coroner studied him, they emptied his pockets into bags, did their studies and put him on a stretcher. The body was taken out. The forensic team was dusting for fingerprints and checking for blood spots, marking things, putting items in evidence bags. As each one completed their job, the area was slowly pout back to almost normal.

"Whomever killed him knew what they were doing," said the coroner to the Sheriff. "He was stabbed in the abdomen, the knife blade sideways and juggled back and forth to cut the main arteries. He bled out in minutes. I don't think here. He was dragged and put here in the church for a reason."

"Any idea of the victim's identity?" asked Troy, finishing up the photos and joining the two officers.

"That's the bank president's father. He usually lives in a home by the lake in Bratenahl - that's a fancy suburb of Cleveland." replied Erick. "He was probably here for Alex's wife Allison's birthday party. Why would someone kill another retiree? He was a good man, I knew him from way back. Always donating to charity, doing fundraisers. Not a mean spot in his body. I've contacted his son and he's on the way over to ID the body before it's shipped to the morgue at the hospital."

"Where were these people in the 1980's" asked Troy.

"Well, Alex was a kid, so his dad was bank president; the other victim would have been teaching Alex algebra over at the high school."

"They're connected somehow." Troy tipped his head over and looked thoughtful. He moved to a center spot, looked towards the back of the church, then the pulpit, then back. "I think he came in that back door to the left. There is no evidence of anything being dragged in, but shine those lights over here, guys, yeah, I thought so, blood spots here and there. Definitely came through that door. Guys here and into the parking lot. We are looking for the murder spot."

"Why was the church hit three times, do you suppose?" asked Brad.

"This is the quilt square," Erick held up an evidence bag. "I wonder which it is in the book?"

"My guess is The House that Jack Built." answered Troy, taking the square. "I sort of recall it from a page in that quilt lady's book."

"Excuse me? What has that got to do with a bank president?" demanded a forensic aide?"

"I got some more info to plug in from the local quilt historian. Let's get back to the office and add all this to the map. I got a bad feeling we're going to see more than we want to before this is over. Brad, just a minute, you're sort of a local historian. What was the name of Mrs. Clarion's ex?" Brad studied a moment and an odd look came over his face. "John Hiram Clamons, I think. He was a salesman of some kind; I'd have to look it up. But I recall as a kid hearing Mrs. Clamons call him Jack."

"This is our first variation to the MO," said Troy. "This square wasn't on the original page of the quilt book. Either we have a copycat, or he's branching into other chapters."

"Which means we could have dozens of crimes from here. There must be hundreds of squares in that book you showed me," replied Erick, frustration showing in his hands clenching and the way he stood straighter and lifted his chin. "Gentlemen we are not going to let that happen in this town. Let's get back to the office and see what we have to do to make this town safe again."

Don't miss the next book of the series coming out soon! **If you enjoy Christian fiction,** you might enjoy the series I completed last year called *The Oberllyn Family Chronicles*. It traces the stories of a single family through three centuries in America, past, present times and future, with an eye on warning all those of us who love liberty and love the Lord what could happen to our freedoms if we don't guard them and pay attention to what is happening. The first book in the Series, <u>The Oberllyns Overland</u>, deals with the family at the time of the Civil war. *Here's the first chapter!*

"Well, mother, it's just about all I can stand," remarked Elijah Oberllyn as he stepped into the kitchen.

"What happened this time?" answered his wife Elizabeth. She was busy rolling out the dough for homemade noodles on the wooden kitchen table. Behind her on the woodstove was bubbling a rich broth to cook them in. From the oven came the wonderful smell of peach pie baking, and warm bread stood on the counter, covered in tea towels. Elizabeth was short woman, with her long black hair, just starting to show grey, done up in a bun at the back of her neck, wearing a solid brown apron over a calico brown dress, and she looked capable of taking on the entire army and feeding it at once. Bustling as she rolled out the dough, she reminded you of a wren on a branch, swaying and hopping from task to task, chirping merrily in between.

"That neighbor Jacks," began her husband. "He's let his cattle get into my wheat again. He says he'll mend the fence but this time he said it was my fault because if I hadn't planted wheat, his cows wouldn't have been tempted, and he is talking about suing me for tempting his cows!"

His wife looked at him and finally said, "You're serious? He is going to try suing you for tempting cows?" She started to laugh out loud but hushed herself when she saw how angry her husband was. "It appears to me the only person to benefit from that would be the lawyers."

"He wants my field to add to his farm. He won't mend the fences on purpose. He's expecting me to do his fence. He's doing the same thing to our son. He offered him a pittance for his orchard, and when Noah wouldn't sell, he started rumors about him being half crazed since the church kicked him out during the great Disappointment and not being right so some of our own neighbors are questioning us for having our own services and I simply am not sure what to do. It's bad enough he picks on us but really, taking off after my son is just about all I can stand." Elizabeth considered for a moment, then said quietly to her husband,

"It's not much of a witness to be fighting with the neighbors. Joe wants to go to California to hunt for gold, but Catherine is not about to drop everything for a wild goose chase. Noah seems content here. I haven't spoken to Mary or Emily about it. I suppose we could consider moving but I hate the idea."

"We've lived here peaceably with our neighbors for years. It's only since those Jacks moved into their uncle's farm we've had trouble. Our land is fertile enough, but when Jacks heard we'd tried to buy his uncle's farm once, he took a dislike to us. And now look." Her husband poured himself a cup of coffee and sat down, blowing on it to cool it, then looking at is wife with a pensive expression on his face.

"California is a right far piece to go," he started.

"Elijah! I was only giving you ideas from different members of the family, not saying I wanted to go." His wife turned with her hands on her hips, a distinctly displeased look on her face.

"It's a good idea and I might have to look into it. I don't want to be run out of town on a rail and that's just what that Jack's fellow is going to try and make happen. Besides, it's getting too crowded around here. It wasn't so bad before that train got put in. Now there are more people coming to buy land and settle in and it's just too crowded."

"Well, you need to pray about anything before you go off half-cocked," she said firmly. "Now go do your chores whilst I finish up supper."

Elijah went back to his barn and finished cleaning out stalls. His wife's jerseys would be up soon for milking. They'd cost him a pretty penny when he'd gotten them, but had proven to be just what Ma's dairy business needed. They gave rich milk, it made wonderful cheese and butter, and their farm was getting known for its good fruit and cheese. Until that neighbor had moved here, everything had been going along fine. Joe had a good thought, though. Out west, there was plenty of land and it wasn't crowded. They could worship as they pleased on Saturday and not be accused of being Judaizers or crazy or anything else. He had two more children at home and there'd be no land to give them as a farm of their own if he couldn't buy up some land. When his son Nathaniel got married, it was a good thing he was a doctor who hadn't time to farm. The farm was just too divided up as it was, what with Emily and her brood, and Catherine and David over by the creek running the small fruits part of the family business. Miriam's man Joe being a lawyer had helped; they'd just needed land for a house and little garden for themselves, no real farming involved. Noah and Mary had taken over the fruit orchard and were making a good go of it, and he and Elizabeth still had enough for him to raise the best horses and oxen in the county and keep mom's dairy running, but they needed more land. It just couldn't be divided anymore and there was Thomas and Johanna yet to be grown and have a part. He supposed Thomas could inherit their home but where would Joanna go? And that Jacks trying to force them to sell land to him they didn't have to spare, he and his dirty tricks. Hard to imagine what he'd try next. Maybe Joe had a good idea. *I believe I'll just visit the land office and find out about land west of here. It surely wouldn't be bad to have a look.*

He came out of the barn and stretched. His son Thomas came dashing up; that child never went anywhere at a walk, always running. "Pa, you got a letter."

"Oh? Thank you, son. Let's have a look." He took the letter from him. It was an official looking document from the US government.

"Haven't seen one of these since well before you were born."

"Was that back when you and mama lived in New York?"

"Yes, pretty much when you were a baby, before grandpa died and we inherited the farm."

"Wonder what they want?"

"Whatever it is, your mom and I will deal with it. You're supposed to have seen to the goats."

"Done. You know the mom angora is going to give birth any day?" he grinned. "Can't wait to see them. I love the way the babies sprong around."

"Well, you keep a good eye on her."

Thomas hesitated. "Pa, I saw Mike Jacks over looking at mom's sheep. He had this funny look on his face?"

"Funny like how?"

"He said his dad doesn't like sheep, they ruin the field. I told him it wasn't his field so not to worry about it. He said something under his breath and walked off. I don't like him much, pa. I was hoping for a friend that would move in that I could do stuff with but I don't think he likes me much."

"Don't worry about him. There are other folks to be with that don't cause such aggravation. Just be civil and leave him be."

"Yes, pa. He made Johanna cry. Oh!" he covered his mouth.

"What?"

"I wasn't supposed to tell you."

"Stop right now. You don't keep secrets from me, ever. When was Johanna crying?"

"She went out to get the cows yesterday and Ellie Jacks was waiting and called her a cowgirl and teased her about her hair."

"What's wrong with her hair?"

"It's sort of red, I guess. And Johanna was crying when she helped with milking."

"I see. And you weren't supposed to tell me?"

"Johanna said we were having enough trouble with this family and God wouldn't want her complaining about it."

"I see. Well, you just let me handle this. Must be about time for supper, yes, there's mom ringing the dinner bell. Let's go wash up."

Dad and Thomas washed up at the pump and went inside, hanging their hats by the door.

"That smell sure chirks a fellow up, ma. Can't wait to have some of your chicken and noodles." Elizabeth smiled.

"Johanna, would you mind getting the field tea I made? I put it in the springhouse to get cold." Johanna nodded and went out the door, coming back with a pitcher covered in a towel.

"Mom," she frowned. "I don't think we ought to use the tea."

"What's the matter?"

"Somebody's been in the spring house."

"Really? How do you know?"

"The cheese's are all on the floor and the milk's spilt."
Ma and Pa rushed outside to the spring house where they
found rounds of cheese scattered all over, the five gallon milk
cans flipped, polluting the spring run over. They looked
around at the damage. Ma shook her head.

"I hate to think we'd have to put guards on our home,
but this is outrageous."

"If we tell the sheriff," began Thomas.

"He'll say it could've been done by animals, that
someone left the door open. There's no proof."

"Why don't we make a list of what's going on at least
and ask him to watch out with us?" asked Ma.

"We can do that. Are the cheeses ruined?"

"The shelves are broken down, but the cheese ought to
be fine. I may have to rewrap some.."

"Let's see what we can do. Thomas - call Mick and
Mike." Mike and Mick were the family mastiffs who spent
most the time in the back field with the cattle. The dogs came
to Thomas's call. "We'd best keep the dogs close to the yard
or at least one of them here."

"Then who's going to protect the cattle from coyotes?"
asked Thomas.

"It's not the four legged ones I am worried about just
now."

Thomas and dad reset the shelves, and they helped
mom wipe off the wax coated cheeses and set them back.
While they did that, mom set the milk cans up and opened the
overflow wide so the water could drain out and run clear.
Finally they stood up and went out. Dad shut the door to the
spring house and set Mike by the door, telling him to stay.
He took Mick to the barn and set him there and they went
inside to eat.

The meal was a quiet one. Ma and Pa were tight-lipped and Thomas and Johanna were quiet as they passed food around.

"I don't care what they say. Johanna, you have got the prettiest hair in the world. It shines in the sun like gold and when you wear your green Sabbath dress I have the prettiest sister in the county."

Johanna looked surprised and her eyes welled up. "Thank you," she whispered.

"I agree with your brother. I am not quite sure why he said it but thank you for noticing," said Pa. Mom and Johanna just looked confused. Suddenly, there was a loud meow from out back.

"What on earth!" said Ma, getting up. She went out back where a strange collie dog had her pet cat up a tree. She took a switch and chased it off. The dog ran to the end of the driveway where Mike Jacks was watching.

"Lady, you'd better not hurt my dog," he yelled at her.

"Then keep him on your own land," she replied.

"Well, this is going to be our land when my dad gets done with you," he yelled back. "You'd better not let those sheep overgraze it." Mom picked up a bigger switch and headed down the drive purposefully in his direction and he ran off. A passing wagon stopped.

"You all right, Mrs. Oberllyn?" said the farmer driving.

"I don't know, Zeb. We got neighbor problems. My spring house was attacked, they insult us and we just never did them any harm."

"I heard about some of that. Mr. Jacks was in the general store last week boasting he'd have your land soon. I don't know what he was talking about but I was coming to tell your husband if he was going to sell out, to call on me. I could use good fields like yours."

"I thank you, and I'll tell Elijah, but we have no interest in leaving our farm. It's been in the family for over a hundred years."

"Thought he might be blowing smoke. But still, keep me and my sons in mind. I'd rather buy from you than Jacks. Oh, and best be careful. There's some weird rumors going around." Elijah was on the porch and waved to his neighbor.

"Rumors?"

"I'm sure they ain't true. You say howdy to Elijah for me."

"Thank you, Zeb. By the way, did he happen to say why he wanted my land?"

"He said it was the best land in the district and I have to agree with him. Your orchards make the best fruit, your cheese is wonderful and you've always been real supportive of our community. Shame to have you leave."

"Aren't planning on leaving."

"I hope not. Well, I best be getting home. You remember my offer."

Mom went to the back where Thomas had climbed the tree and gotten her Maine coon cat down. He jumped into her arms. "There, there, dear. I'm sorry he flustered you so. Shh, now. Shhh."

"Mom, why do they hate us?"

"I have no idea." They went inside. "We've never had this much trouble."

"Mom, did you know Jacks have got slaves?"

"What?"

"They have three of them. I saw them out working his field. And Mr. Jacks carries a whip."

"I see. Well, the good Lord never wanted slavery. We earn our needs by the works of our hands, not the sweat of others. Let's try to finish supper. It's most likely all cold by now."

About the Author:

J. Traveler Pelton was born in West Virginia in the last century. She served as Nation's Mother for her tribe, for six years. She is wife to Dan (45 years!), mother of six adults, a grandmother of eight, a Clinically Licensed Independent Social Worker with Supervisory Status, at present in private practice, a retired adjunct professor of social work at her local university and an insatiable reader. She is a cancer survivor. Traveler avidly studies science and technology, fascinated by the inventiveness of people. She is quick to draw parallels in different fields and weave stories around them. Traveler is a fabric artist and her most enjoyable time is spent spinning yarn while spinning yarns for the grandkids.

You can reach Traveler at her website: **travelerpelton.com**

Or like us and share us on **Facebook at Traveler Pelton**

Or write to her by **snail mail** at

Springhaven Croft
216 Sychar Rd.
Mt. Vernon, OH 43050

She loves to hear from her readers!

All our books are available on Amazon as both eBook and print copy, Kindle unlimited as free downloads

We'd love it if you'd leave us a review! It helps others find our books.

God bless and see you in our next travels together!

Your Attention Please!!!!

<u>Would you like to join the team at Potpourri Books?</u>

Traveler is <u>always</u> looking for responsible beta readers for her new books. A beta reader gets a prepublication copy of all new books, <u>free of charge</u> in exchange for an honest review written on Amazon, and a short email letting her know of any glitches you may have found that got past the editor, any suggestions you may have, and your opinion of the book. What else do you get out of it?

A beta reader gets:
A free download of one of her already published books and as soon as your review of that book gets placed on Amazon, free downloads of her already published works: for each review, you get a free book.
And
A free copy pre-publication copy of all new books…
And
Other neat freebies as they come, from bookmarks to stickers to posters to pens to neat things I find to send out to my betas-
Interested?
Contact Traveler at
<u>travelerpelton@gmail.com</u> for more info…

We would love to add you to the team!

Blessings for you:

Dear Lord,
Give me a few friends
who will love me for what I am,
and keep ever burning
before my vagrant steps
the kindly light of hope...
And though I come not within sight
of the castle of my dreams,
teach me to be thankful for life,
and for time's olden memories
that are good and sweet.
And may the evening's twilight
find me gentle still.

Old Celtic blessing....

I've seen better days, but I've also seen worse.
I don't have everything that I want, but I do have all I need.
I woke up with some aches and pains, but I woke up.
My life may not be perfect, but I am blessed."
Anonymous

Until you join me on another journey, may you be blessed as well!